Celebrity Dish

M.R. ANGLIN

CHAPTER 1

Jessica's new hit song, "Pay Attention to Me," blared from a radio sitting on a shelf in a restaurant on the Boardwalk.

Xena had never related to a song more.

The teenage vixen sat on a wooden bench outside the eatery. She was supposed to be on a date with her boyfriend, a fox named Hunter; but instead he sat beside her with one foot on the bench, amber eyes glued to his laptop computer screen and his portable, palm-sized printer sitting beside him. Out of the printer came long strips of narrow paper that looked like credit card receipts.

Xena crossed her arms and glared at him. His long, sandy hair faded to a shade of pinkish-purple at the ends and had been pulled back into a ponytail. In that way, they matched. Her dull, black hair was in a ponytail too, but while his was tight and neat, hers was a bit messy, the ends curling up. Hunter's tail twitched as he worked, a sign of great concentration, and his large ears dotted with earrings remained still. He wore board shorts and a white T-shirt—a perfect match to the beach stretching out below the Boardwalk.

"I sure am having a good time, Hunter," Xena said much louder than she needed to. "I'm so glad I dropped everything to go out with you today."

"Uh, huh," Hunter said.

Xena clenched her teeth. "And I'd have even more fun if we were *doing* something!"

"Uh, huh." Hunter tapped on the keyboard. "Give me something. Come on!" he muttered.

"Hunter!" Xena shot to her feet. "I said you could work on your computer for five minutes. It's been close to an hour!"

"Just a second, Xena." Hunter held up a finger at her. "I'm almost done. Five more minutes."

Xena plopped back on the bench, crossed her arms, and gazed up at the sky. It seemed that the Isle de Losierres, the island where she and her family were staying, never had a cloudy day. The sun beamed down and reflected off of her fur, casting shimmering light patterns on the bench beside her. She tried to cover her arms and legs, but it was impossible with the spaghetti strap shirt and the jeans shorts she wore. They were a comfortable choice, but they left her fur exposed. She hadn't known that even though she wore an image-generator to make her pelt look dull gray, the sun would still reflect off of its real color: silver. She had a genetic condition that caused her fur to store high amounts of metals. That, in turn, allowed her to manipulate electricity. Her condition was also why she and her family were on the Isle. They were in hiding from those who would capture her or to use her abilities to harm others.

Good thing Hunter had come into her life. He was a certified Silver Fox Trainer—the only one in the world. And he taught her how to keep her electricity under control . . . when he wasn't obsessed with his job.

She sighed and tried to lean back in the shade of the awning. The ocean shimmered blue and green as white-capped waves crashed on the yellow sand. Even early in the morning—it must have been 9 or so—sunbathers dotted the sand with colorful swimsuits and punctuated the rush of the ocean with laughter. The ever-growing crowd tramping on the Boardwalk chattered as they window-shopped or enjoyed early-morning snacks in shaded cafés.

"Of course *I* got a ticket. I'm surprised *you* did!"

Xena recognized Shandra's voice floating through the air. The tigress stood a few feet away holding at least five shopping bags. Dori, a chameleon; Mira, a wolf; and Katie, a raccoon, stood around her.

"I got my ticket this morning." Dori turned a warm shade of satisfactory yellow.

"You had to have been at the bottom of the list, then," Shandra sniffed, her nose up in the air. "And no wonder after what you showed up in to that premier party.”

Xena glanced at Hunter, grunted, and then dashed over to her friends. She took a moment to check that her image-generator was working before she greeted them. The last thing she wanted was for them to find out about her fur. In her experience, no one wanted to be friends with a freak. “Hi, guys.”

“Xena, hi.” Mira stepped away from the circle to greet her. She had brown fur, brown hair with frosted highlights, and olive-green eyes. The make-up she wore today enhanced the silkiness of her fur and the contour of her rounded cheeks, but Xena noted she had applied a different shade of eyeshadow for each eye—to compensate for the light patch she had around her left eye.

“What are you doing here?” Mira looked around. “I thought you were on a date.”

“I am, or at least, I’m supposed to be.” Xena shot a look at him. “He’s too busy on his computer to even notice that I left,” she shouted to him.

“One second, one second, Xena,” Hunter said, and Xena had to strain to hear him over the beach noise. “Almost done.”

Xena threw her hands in the air. “I don’t know what to do with him. He’s been ignoring me lately—cancelling dates, forgetting to call. I don’t know why he’s acting this way.” Her ears fell. “I can’t think of anything I did wrong.”

Shandra studied her up and down. “It’s gotta be your clothes.”

“What’s wrong with my clothes?”

“You’d get a quicker response if you asked what’s right with them,” Dori said, curling and uncurling her tail.

“You looked like you just got out of bed.” Katie tossed her large, striped tail to the side.

“She’s right.” Mira tilted her head to the side. “You and I need to go on a shopping spree and get you some nice things. You have to stop raiding my mother’s old closet.” She snapped Xena’s shirt strap.

Xena stepped back out of Mira’s reach. “But it was your idea. You said since I’m staying in your mom’s old house that I could borrow her things because the style suited me.”

“I didn’t mean for you to use them exclusively.” Mira swung her shopping back around. “I thought you’d get your own clothes by now. What happened to the stuff I bought you when you got on the Isle?”

"I wear them, and I *did* go buy more things." Xena extended her hands. "These are all mine."

Mira hissed in a breath through her teeth. "I was hoping they looked like that because they were old . . ."

"Point is, you can*not* keep a guy like Hunter dressed like that." Shandra used her index finger to point at Xena's clothes.

"You have to dress for success." Dori pouted like a model on a magazine cover.

"Guys have short attention spans, Xena." Shandra placed a hand on her shoulder. "You have to give them something to pay attention to."

"Um . . ." Xena rubbed her arm. "That sounds good in theory, but I don't want to wear low-cut shirts or super-short skirts. I don't like the look, and I don't feel comfortable in it. Hunter's going to have to use his imagination." Her ears pricked then she blushed and giggled. "But not too much."

"Xena, Xena, Xena . . ." Mira put an arm around her. "We're not talking about baring all here. We're talking about being fabulous. Am I right girls?"

"Duh," Shandra said. "Look at us!"

They all struck a pose. Shandra showed off her maroon, sleeveless dress; Mira wore a purple three-quarter sleeve shirt and a dark green skirt; Dori donned a white T-shirt with lace on the edges and blue jeans that hugged her curves; and Katie was wearing a sleeveless white jumpsuit that fell mid-thigh.

Xena nodded. "Point taken."

"Tell you what." Mira let her arm slide off of Xena's shoulder. "After Jessica's trip to the Isle, we'll all take you shopping to find your own personal, fabulo style."

"Oh, yes!" Shandra spun in a circle and making her bags twirl. "This is my dream come true—a chance to challenge my fashion acumen in order to make something presentable out of you."

"We're going to have so much fun." Katie hopped in place.

"Wait, wait, wait! Back up!" Xena waved her hands as if to clear the air. "Did you say Jessica is coming? Here?" She squealed. "I love Jessica!"

"You and everyone else," Dori said.

Shandra twirled her hair. "Don't act like a noob while she's here. You'll embarrass us all."

"She's performing a concert at the end of stay," Dori waved a piece of paper in the air. "And guess who got her ticket," she sang.

"A concert?" Xena cocked her head. "But isn't that sort of a fan thing? I thought you didn't do events like that on the Isle."

"We don't; not usually, but . . ." Mira placed a hand on her chest. "I happen to be a huge Jessica fan, and since she was desperate to visit the Isle last minute, I got my mother to make putting on a concert a condition of her stay."

"Plus, she's not performing *on* the Isle." Shandra twitched her tail in disgust. "That's too . . . common for us."

"I'd never allow that. Can you imagine allowing just anyone access the Isle for the price of a ticket?" Mira shuddered. "That would undermine the very thing that makes us so special."

Xena let one of her ears flatten. "And what's that?"

"Oh, I know." Katie waved her hand in the air. "Exclusivity!"

"It's super important." Mira nodded gravely.

"Sounds prejudiced to me," Xena muttered.

Mira fell silent a moment. She trapped her bottom lip with her index finger. "I see what you mean—excluding people doesn't seem very nice, but if it wasn't for that, you wouldn't be able to hide here. Our exclusive nature is what allows people to remain anonymous on the Isle. And celebrities pay a mint for having a place where no one swamps them all the time."

"I guess . . ." Xena held her hands behind her back.

"But, honestly, I didn't think Jessica would agree to my condition." Mira leaned in close, and everyone leaned in to hear her next statement. "She's paying through the nose for a huge suite, and she's not taking nearly as many people as stars usually bring the first time they come on vacation. She's only bringing four or five. We could have easily fit her entire entourage in her suite if she wanted."

"What's a normal entourage?" Xena asked.

Mira thought for a moment. "20-40."

Xena's eyes widened. "That many?"

"But most stars leave the Isle realizing they don't need all that fuss. Their next go around is much more reasonable. In any case, since Jessica agreed to the concert, she'll be singing there." Mira pointed across the sea to the west. "See that hazy blue across the ocean? That's the Losierres Concert Hall. The whole island is one big stadium. It's where we do all our concert-like events. It's the closest most people ever get to setting foot on the Isle."

"And to keep it more exclusive, tix are super-expensive." Shandra clasped her hands. "Ah, exclusivity. I love it."

"I see." Xena played with the sand that had been blown in by the wind. "How do you get tickets, and how expensive are they? Maybe if I sit at the very last row and beg my dad, he'll spring for them."

The girls, except Mira, burst into laughter, their noses high in the air.

"If you have to ask," Shandra held her hand under her nose, "you're not getting any."

"Tickets are already sold out. I tried to reserve one for you, but they went too quickly." Mira caught Xena's hands. "I'm sorry. I couldn't even save one for my new boyfriend."

"Boyfriend?" Xena's ears pricked.

"Oh, boy." Shandra rolled her eyes. "Here she goes again."

"Don't be jealous because I got me a new man." Mira tossed her hair at Shandra. "He is so fine and so sweet. I can't wait to introduce you."

"And I can't wait to meet him." Xena squeezed Mira's hands.

"Xena." Hunter walked up to her. "Why'd you walk off like that?" He slipped his hand around her shoulder before nodding to her friends. 'Sup, ladies."

"Hi, Hunter," they chimed, batting their eyes.

Xena shrugged his hand off. "I'm not talking to you, Hunter." She thrust her nose in the air

Hunter stared at her, his ears flicking back. "Why?"

"I can't tell you; I'm not talking to you."

Hunter leaned in so close that his growing whiskers tickled her face. "You are right now. So, come on. Tell me what's wrong."

"Fine, I will." Xena jabbed his chest with her index finger. "I told you that you could work on your computer for five minutes, and it's been over an hour!"

Hunter glanced at his watch and winced. Then he glowered at her, his tail bristling. "If I was taking so long, why didn't you tell me? I'm not a mind-reader, you know."

"I did tell you! Several times!" Xena balled up her fists as she shouted, "You weren't listening to me!"

"Oh." Hunter took a step back. He fell silent, gazing at the wooden planks that made up the Boardwalk. "I'm sorry, Xena. I didn't realize."

Xena pinched her lips together and turned her back on him.

"Please forgive me." Hunter stepped up beside her to look at her face.

She turned again.

"Please, Xena." He placed his hands on her shoulders. "I'll buy you something real nice to make up for it."

"If you think you can buy my forgiveness—"

"I'll get you a lollipop from that candy store you like . . . I know they're your favorite."

Xena looked at him out of the corner of her eye. She *did* like lollipops.

"I really am sorry, Xena." Hunter hung his head and looked at her with wide eyes. "I had to get this done by noon. I had no idea that I was ignoring you. I know a lollipop can't make up for it, but take it as a promise that it will never happen again." He smiled at her, revealing a row of slightly crooked teeth. "Please."

A smile cracked Xena's angry façade. "What kind of lollipop?"

"Whatever you want."

"Why don't you go and get it, and I'll decide if it's acceptable when you come back."

"Don't move, okay?" Hunter kissed her on the cheek and darted to the Sugar Shop.

"He's good." Dori turned a shade of reddish-pink with a hint of purple in it.

"He made me want to forgive him." Mira laid a hand on her chest.

"I'm melting over here." Katie fanned herself.

Shandra snorted through her nose. "I totally would have held out for more."

"Absolutely," Mira said.

Xena's eyes widened. "You think I could have gotten two lollipops out of him?"

"Forget the lollipops, Xena!" Mira caught her by the shoulders. "I'm talking about designer clothes."

"Expensive jewelry," Dori said.

"High-end purses. Hello!" Shandra said.

"I wouldn't feel right accepting things like that from Hunter." Xena glanced in the direction of the candy store. "Lollipops are one thing, but I'm fifteen years old. What am I going to do with expensive jewelry and high-end purses?"

The girls gawked at her as if she had spontaneously combusted.

"Xena." Mira picked up her hand and patted it. "I am so glad that you came here when you did. Uncle J.R. must have had you so sheltered. But don't worry; we'll have your priorities straightened out in no time."

"Um . . . I don't see anything wrong with my priorities." Xena pulled her hand from Mira's grasp.

"And that's the problem." Mira pretended to wipe tears from her eyes. "No cousin of mine will grow up socially inept."

Xena looked at Mira. Their eyes met, and they burst into laughter.

"I still don't get how you two are cousins." Katie looked from one to the other. "Neither of you look like you're wolf-fox hybrids."

"It's easy." Mira pressed her cheek to Xena's. "My mother is her father's sister."

Katie gazed at her, her brows furrowing. "But . . . I . . ."

"My sister and I are adopted." Xena pulled away from Mira. "Sort of."

Dori nodded. "That makes more sense."

"Here you go, Zizzie." Hunter handed her a lollipop that was half the size of her head.

"Hunter, thank you! I—" She caught him staring at his portable printer. "I can't believe you are working again!"

"No, no, no." Hunter waved his hand. "Wait till you see what I'm printing off for you. This is good."

"It had better be." Xena gripped the lollipop stick so hard that it started to crack.

Hunter tore off the piece of paper. "Ta-da!" He presented it to her.

Xena snatched it from him and glanced at it. She gasped. "A will call receipt for the Concert Hall's box office? Are these tickets to Jessica's performance?"

"I couldn't get any." Hunter let his ears fall. "They're all sold out. All I could get are . . ." He grinned. ". . . backstage passes."

"Whoa!" The girls gathered around her.

Xena screeched. "Thank you, Hunter." She threw her arms around him. "Thank you. You are the best boyfriend ever."

"Don't thank me yet." Hunter pulled her off of him. "That's sort of a bribe."

Xena let her tail flop on the floor. "A bribe for what?"

"I wanted to get all the information I needed for my next job over the computer, but the client's being difficult and wants me to meet her in person." Hunter rubbed the back of his head. "Today. In fifteen minutes."

Xena slumped her shoulders. "Are you kidding?"

"It's only for a little bit, Xena, I promise. You can come with me. You'll like this client, and we'll be in and out in no time. And we'll do whatever you want afterward; I promise." Hunter laced his fingers. "Please."

Xena let her hands drop to her sides. "Hunter, you said we'd hang out. You've been so busy lately . . ."

"I know, but this job is really, really important, and it won't take long. After this, I'm all yours." Hunter took her hands. "Please."

Xena sighed, letting her eyes fall to the Boardwalk. "I guess."

"Thank you." Hunter pulled her into a tight hug. "I owe you big time. I'm going to get my stuff, and we'll be off."

Xena watched him trot back to the bench. Her eyes dropped to the receipt. Backstage passes didn't seem so exciting now.

"Wow. Backstage passes." Mira put a hand on her shoulder. "That's the kind of thing I would have held out for." She gave her a sympathetic smile.

"There is hope for you, after all." Shandra tossed her hair. "Though, I wouldn't have let him go—ow!" She rubbed her shoulder where Mira elbowed her. "I better not bruise, Mira." She thrust her nose in the air and marched off. Katie and Dori scurried after her with a wave goodbye to Xena.

"See you, later, Xena." Mira gave her Xena's shoulder a squeeze. "Let me know how it turns out, but I'm sure it'll be fine."

"Thanks."

Mira winked before jogging off to catch up with the others. She watched as they all disappeared into the crowd.

"Where'd the girls go?" Hunter walked up to her with his things in a backpack slung over his shoulder.

"Shopping."

"Then let's head off." Hunter took her hand and led her down the boardwalk. "You won't regret this."

"I hope not." Xena said and let him lead her away.

CHAPTER 2

Just off the Isle, on the mainland, a hover-limo approached a dock. It was followed by five other hover-cars and SUVs. A crowd of screaming people with signs in hand waited to greet them. Inside the limo sat two figures lounging on the leather seats. One was a tan mongoose and the other a bird of . . . indeterminate species. She had the yellow feathers of a canary, but her tail had the shape of an ostrich's. Those tail feathers filled the seat so that the mongoose sat tilted toward the door. The feathers on her head curled and swirled around her face, and a crest of three feathers extended beyond them. She had the curved beak of a red-tailed hawk. Her arms—wings, really—rested on her lap. She wore a red, asymmetrical dress that grazed her upper thigh. The dress was so short that Alex, the mongoose, feared that any movement would show of her . . . "treasures" . . . so he insisted she wear black tights underneath. At first Jessica had resisted, but after seeing how nicely the black contrasted with her high-heeled, thigh-high red boots, she took it as her idea. The entire outfit, excluding the tights, had been covered with sequins that glittered in the light.

It made Alex' head hurt.

"I cannot wait to get onto the Isle and out of this thing." Jessica tapped her phone with long pin-feathers that served as fingers.

"We're at the dock now, Jessica." Alex watched her fingers fly over the screen. "Who are you texting?"

"Just a fan." Jessica placed her phone face down on her lap.

"Considering our problem, Jessica, it may not be wise to cavort with fans right now." Alex pointed out. "And you shouldn't be giving out your private number to fans anyway."

"Stop trying to be my mother." Jessica turned to the window.

Alex stifled a groan. Being the manager to a star like Jessica wasn't easy. But the pay was nice.

The limo pulled to a stop. Alex peered past Jessica to gaze at the clear, blue ocean. The sun sparkled off of the waves lapping on rocks underneath the dock. Lovely water but no beach to speak of. All that was reserved for the Isle's visitors. At the end of the dock stood a wooden building. A path was marked off by a red carpet and stanchions, and on either side of the carpet a crowd pushed and shoved each other to get a glimpse of the limo and its occupants.

"I love fans." Jessica waved at the crowd through the window. "But it'll be nice to get out and walk around without being mobbed."

"That is precisely what the Isle offers." Alex made some last minute scheduling adjustments on his phone. "It took me some serious finagling to get us there this week."

"Anyone else could have done it quicker." Jessica turned her beak up. "And without forcing me to do a concert."

"It was your idea to agree to that." Alex clenched his teeth. "And I had no idea you did until after the fact."

"That's because you couldn't seem to get the job done." Jessica clacked her beak the way she always did when annoyed. Alex heard that noise a lot. "And why aren't all my bodyguards and stylists and choreographers and trainers allowed on?"

"I couldn't get authorization for your usual 30 people entourage, Jess." Alex heaved a deep sigh to calm himself. "The Isle only has so much room. Anyway, you won't need all those people."

Jessica snorted. "I assume the Isle is safe, bearing in mind our problem?"

"Perfectly safe, Jess." Alex waved his phone. "The Isle has the best security of anyone, anywhere. By the time your vacation is over, you'll never have to worry about anything again."

"You had better be right, Alex." Jessica slipped her bare hands into a long-sleeved gloves—red and covered in sequins. The girl had a weakness for sparkle. "And don't call me 'Jess' again."

Jessica's chauffeur opened the door, letting in the ocean breeze. She took a deep breath and stepped out of the car. The crowd roared in screams.

"Hello, everyone!" Jessica strode down the red carpet, blowing kisses at the crowd.

Alex hefted himself out of the limo and stretched his cramped legs. A reporter had caught Jessica's attention so she stood near the building, chatting with her.

"Oh, boy!" Alex rolled his eyes. "We agreed not to do interviews today."

"You know Jessica, Alex." Taylor, a flop-eared, gray rabbit, stepped beside him. "She can't resist the spotlight."

"I hope she doesn't say anything stupid." Alex strode down the carpet.

"—that you're putting on a concert at the end of your stay," the reporter was saying. She was a Russian blue cat that had curly, yellow hair with a pink streak running through it. Alex narrowed his eyes . . . what was her name again? Ah, Stayf, right. She was the head reporter for Celebrity Dish, *the* source for entertainment news. No wonder Jessica stopped to speak with her.

"That's right." Jessica placed her hand on her chest. "It's an exclusive, sold-out concert on the Isle's Concert Hall that will be simulcast to the rest of the world."

Alex slid in front of the mic. "With a 15 second delay. We are legally obligated to mention that."

"Thank you, Alex." Jessica bumped him out of the way and punctuated it with a look that said, "Stay out of my way."

"My sources indicate that you will be unveiling a new look at that concert," Stayf continued as if nothing had happened.

"Absolutely." Jessica gave a dazzling smile. "As you know, my costumes always feature elements from the amazing bird species that live in the world. This time my costume is inspired by . . ." She paused to build up suspense. "The spatuletail hummingbird . . ."

A roar went up from the crowd as all the hummingbirds screamed.

". . . the fantastic and flamboyant peacock . . ."

Another roar from the crowd as peacocks waved their tails.

". . . and the female Regianna bird of paradise!"

A veritable scream from the crowd.

"The audience agrees that it sounds magnificent." Stayf waved the crowd into relative silence. "And what about color?"

"I can't say much else about my new look, Stayf, but I will say this:" Jessica clasped her finger-feathers. "I saw the most amazing thing on television the other day: Expermia! Those peoples' two-toned hair are absolutely mesmerizing. So I incorporated that look into my outfit."

Stayf stared at her for a moment, and the crowd's roar died down to a whisper. "Uh . . . Jessica . . . considering what's happening in Expermia, including the continued devastation being caused by our military in that country, don't you think making a costume out of the Expermian people might be seen as insensitive and ill-timed?"

"What's happening in Expermia?" Jessica blinked for a moment. "Oh, you mean that war? Pfft. No one cares about that anymore."

Alex shot forward to the mic. "Which is why Jessica has decided to bring back some attention to it . . . through her costume."

"Oh! That's right!" Jessica shoved him away. "I was . . . about to say that."

Alex rolled his eyes.

"That's very forthright of you, Jessica." Stayf gave Alex a knowing look. "One more question if you don't mind."

"Anything for you, Stayf." Jessica gave a fetching smile.

"My sources tell me that your sudden visit to the Isle has something to do with unknown parties becoming very close to unmasking you. Is there any truth to that?"

Jessica's eyes widened. "What? . . . I . . . um . . ."

"Sorry, Stayf." Alex slid close to Jessica. "We have a schedule to keep. Jessica."

"Sorry, darling." Jessica smiled at Stayf. "It appears I'm out of time."

"Right. Well, we all wish you a wonderful vacation." Stayf turned to the audience. "Don't we?"

The crowd roared.

"I love you all! Don't forget to watch my concert this Friday!" Jessica waved at them before Alex dragged her into the building. "I love fans."

"I know," Alex said, releasing her arm.

"Greetings," said a seagull standing at the door. He was dressed in a blue and green uniform. "Welcome to the Isle de Losierres Customs Department. Documents, please."

Alex handed him a packet of papers. The inside of the Customs Department was filled with stanchions quartering off lines. Full body scanners stood like arches in the middle of the room.

"Very good," the seagull said after shifting through the papers. "There are to be no electronics or image capturing equipment of any kind brought onto the Isle without a permit. No weapons or image-generators, period. Please step through the scanner to be scanned for such items."

It didn't take long for them to make it through security, though Jessica did have to remove her image-generator. But since most of her costume was physical, the only change anyone saw was in her beak. It was now longer and less curved than before.

She and Alex emerged from the building and stepped out onto the dock behind the building. A long expanse of ocean stretched out before them, and a flight of stairs led straight to the water.

"What is this?" Jessica gazed at the churning sea beneath the dock. "Where's the boat that will take us to the Isle? I am not swimming there, Alex."

"There is no boat, Jessica." Alex watched as one by one, the staff approved to join Jessica on the Isle emerged from the building and joined them on the dock. There was Taylor, her stylist; Drift, her bodyguard, a wolverine; Fred, her lawyer, a blue heron; and then Hans, her fitness coach, a leopard.

"Then how are we supposed to get there?" Jessica pouted.

"Watch." Alex studied where the steps met the water.

The ocean bubbled and writhed as something surfaced, spraying Jessica with mist. A long bridge spanning the ocean emerged. Water cascaded off its edge. After most of the water drained off, high pressured fans blew it dry.

"Are we going to *walk*?" Jessica said.

Alex didn't answer. He climbed down the stairs and stepped onto the bridge.

"I can't believe they expect me to walk." Jessica trod onto the bridge beside him. "You should have planned better, Alex. A nice boat, for instance—"

"A boat would sink." Alex watched Jessica's entourage join them on the bridge. "There are coral reefs surrounding the Isle.

The only way across is by bridge or helicopter, and the Isle only uses helicopters in case of emergency."

"How far is it to the Isle?" Taylor hefted Jessica's make-up bag.

"About three miles." Alex took the bag from her. The rest of their luggage, including Jessica's 10 suitcases, would be waiting for them at the hotel. Thankfully.

Jessica looked up at the wolverine. "I don't suppose you will carry me if I get tired, Drift?"

Drift lifted the corner of his mouth. "No."

Jessica sniffed. "It's a good thing you're a decent bodyguard."

"No one will have to carry anyone," Alex held on to the railing when a single horn blasted. "Hang on to the side."

Everyone did, except Jessica.

"Why?" Jessica said.

The bridge lurched forward. Jessica toppled into Drift's arms.

"That's why." Alex bit his lips together to hide a smile.

"Not funny." Jessica righted herself. "But moving walkway. Much better. I approve."

"Step over here." Alex pulled her to the side. "Chairs will be coming to us soon, and we'll have catch them—like a ski lift."

Jessica watched as a seat rolled by in the center of the walkway. It was followed by several others. She hopped between seats and sat. "Comfy." She slid her arms behind her head. "I think I'll like the Isle."

Alex caught his own seat. A grin spread across his lips. If all went well his and Jessica's problem would be over by the time they left the glorious Isle de Losierres. He couldn't wait to get this vacation started.

CHAPTER 3

"So, Hunter." Xena gave him a look. "Who's your client?"

"You'll see." Hunter's grin had not left his face since they had arrived. Xena snorted through her nose. It was like he didn't notice, or care, that she was still angry. She turned away from him and examined the hotel room he had taken her to.

It was on the top floor of the Rizzon, the most luxurious hotel on the Isle. They were waiting in the parlor, the first of many rooms in the suite that covered the entire fourteenth floor. Portraits of celebrities that had stayed in that room—the most famous of which was Marion McCartney, a white mink that had graced the silver screen in its heyday—hung on the light gray walls. The newest painting featured Jessica in her blue jay, blue bird, and dove inspired costume.

Hunter sat in a pink armchair embroidered with flowers. Light yellow—almost white—curtains flowed over windows that overlooked the sea. The area mats were white and fluffy, and as Xena paced her feet sunk into it. Another sofa faced the window.

"I've never seen anything like this." Xena gazed at the crystal chandelier above, forgetting her anger for the moment. "Whoever booked this place must be rich."

Hunter leaned back in his chair. "Everyone who sets foot on the Isle is rich, Zizzie." He sunk back even further. "Sooo . . . soft!"

"I don't know why I agreed to come here." Xena thrust out her bottom lip. "I am not having fun standing alone!"

"She *is* running late." Hunter glanced at his phone. "Typical. But when you meet her, you'll forgive me."

"That is becoming less and less certain as time goes on." Xena tapped her foot on the carpet.

"Unacceptable, Alex!" A high-pitched, somewhat whiney voice, sounded from outside the door.

"Yes, Jessica," came a voice sounding like it needed a good 24 hour nap. "I'll fix it." The door opened. A mongoose stepped in. He stopped short when he saw Xena and Hunter. "Who are you?" His green eyes narrowed.

Hunter hefted himself out of his seat. "Name's Prowler. Meetin' a client."

Xena gazed at Hunter. His voice had dropped deeper and became more clipped than usual. His eyes seemed to slant more, and his lip had a constant curl to them. Even his ears angled back a bit. It was almost as if someone had flipped a switch and turned his personality inside out.

"What client?" The mongoose stood at the door to block entry for the people behind him. "Get out of here, now!"

"What is the hold up?" A yellow bird shoved the mongoose in. "Stop standing in the doorway, Alex."

Xena's mouth dropped open. "Jessica?" She slapped her hands on her cheeks. "You're Jessica! I can't believe it!" She squealed and danced on her tippy-toes.

Jessica pinched her beak together. "What is this? I thought there weren't supposed to be fans on the Isle. Some high-level security."

"Chill it, girl." Hunter nudged Xena with his elbow. "Ya gatta act more profreshonael."

"Pro . . . fresh . . ." Xena let one of her ears drop. She had to say the word to herself three times before she realized he meant "professional."

"Name's Prowler." Hunter tipped an imaginary hat to Jessica. "Nice to peep ya, chickie."

"H Prowler?" Jessica sniffed. "I thought I'd have time to settle in before you came."

Hunter's grin disappeared. "That 'cause ya late."

Jessica just shrugged.

"You hired a bounty hunter?" Alex turned Jessica around. "Why would you do that?"

"Bounty hunter?" Xena said to herself. She turned to Hunter. His expression had not changed.

"You weren't making any progress to solving my problem, so I decided to handle it myself." Jessica shoved his hands from her shoulder. "You all may leave now. I'll talk to him alone."

"But, Jessica—"

"Leave!" Jessica's body feathers rose, but the ones on her head—except the three feathers that made up her crest—remained motionless. "And get me a latte."

"Fine." Alex ushered Jessica's entourage to the next room. He took one more look at them and closed the door behind him.

Once they were gone, Jessica turned her head to examine Hunter with one eye, a habit Xena had seen with other birds before. "You can't be H Prowler. I'm barely older than you are."

Hunter chuckled, sending shivers up Xena's spine. That laugh felt cold and mirthless. "I find it hilari that everyone I meet think dis my true form," he said. "I choose the one that suits me, chickie."

"Stop calling me 'chickie.' It's demeaning." Jessica put her hands on her hips. "Besides, image-generators aren't allowed on this island, Prowler."

"They ain't for them that can't smuggle 'em." Hunter put his weight on one foot. "'Sides, I got permits."

"I was told no image-generators—permitted or not."

Hunter waved her off. "You dunno the right peeps."

"How do I know you're not lying?"

Hunter tapped his phone. His appearance morphed from fox to raccoon in three seconds. He had a chunk of one ear missing and a tail that was half the size of his body. He tapped it again, and he morphed into a brown rabbit. Again and grew into a tall, slender otter. "And I got more 'sides." He returned to his fox form.

Xena gazed at him. For a moment, she had no idea if the fox she knew was the real Hunter.

"Clearly I need better people on my team." Jessica snorted through her nostrils.

"If yous satisfied, can we get it on?" Hunter plopped in his chair. "I's in a rush."

"Not until I know who she is." Jessica turned her glare to Xena.

For a moment as Hunter turned to Xena, his eyes softened. But it was gone in a second like the sun hidden behind a cloud. "That's my gi—uh, my assistant. More like a-prentice. Doing a favor for a bud; promised to show her the ropes. Name's Zed."

Assistant? Apprentice? Xena shot a glare at Hunter.

"Zed, huh?" Jessica examined Xena up and down. "Nice stage name."

"Um, thanks." A grin spread on Xena's face. "I'm sorry for my reaction earlier, but it is nice to meet you. I'm a huge fan."

Jessica chuckled. "Who isn't?"

"Enough girly-gab." Hunter leaned forward in the chair. "Why is I here?"

"I have . . . a unique problem." Jessica collapsed on the sofa. "As you know, I am an international superstar who gets inspiration for my over-the-top, costumes from all over the globe. No one knows my true species, and that's by design. I don't want them to know."

"Why?" Xena sat beside her.

"That is not your business." Jessica tossed a magazine on the glass table between the chair and the sofa. It featured her image in a pink and purple flamingo inspired costume with the word "EXPOSED" stamped over it. "The mystery surrounding my costumes has become something of a sensation. Tabloids, and even national and international news outlets, are all trying to get the scoop on my true identity. Every time they think they've figured it out, I get free publicity."

"Nice scam." Hunter picked up the magazine.

"I know, right?" Jessica crossed her legs. "It's worked out better than I could have dreamed. Sometimes I even bait them on purpose with 'leaks' when I need an extra boost in the public eye."

"Publicity stunt." Hunter had opened the magazine and was reading an article.

"Exactly, except . . . lately someone's gotten too close to the truth." Jessica's smile faded. "They could figure out who I am and expose me. Do you know how that feels?"

Xena ducked her head. She rubbed her arms and pictured Mira or Shandra discovering her fur—the gasping, the disgusted looks. It made her stomach twist. "I understand."

"What's dat gotta do wit me?" Hunter kept reading.

"I've been getting these." Jessica tossed an envelope on the table.

Hunter opened it. Inside were several letters. Xena moved to his armrest to read them over his shoulder.

> Dear Jessica,
> I'm your biggest fan. I love your work, and I love you. Keep it up.
> Dan.

"Sounds like an ordinary fan letter to me," Xena said.
Jessica wrung her feather-fingers. "Keep reading."

> Dear Jessica,
> I love you. I know your song, "Love Me Forever," was meant for me. Will you marry me?
> Dan.

"This is getting weird," Xena said as Hunter flipped to the next letter.

> Dear Jessica,
> Why don't you answer my letters, calls, and emails? I know you're only dating Bruce Charles to make me jealous. You don't have to do that. Don't you know that I love you? And I'm waiting for the time when you wise up, dump Bruce, and come back to me.
> Dan.

> Dear Jessica,
> You were so beautiful sleeping last night. I couldn't help taking a souvenir from you. Your hair ribbon smells as sweet as you do. I sleep with it and dream of you. I left you a gift. Enjoy.
> Dan.

"He broke into your house?" Xena hopped to her feet. "What a whack job!"

"It's got me really scared. I've gone through three bodyguards in the last five months, but he still gets close." Jessica tapped her beak together. "The police said that incident where he broke in was probably a prank from one of my friends since they found no signs of forced entry. And that ribbon he referred to was found the next day on my dresser." Her brows furrowed. "But the thing is, I don't sleep in my costume. Prank or not, it's disturbing to me . . . especially when you move on to the last letter."

Hunter shuffled through until he came to it:

> Dear Jessica,
> You continue to snub me though I have pledged my love for you over and over. What do I have to do to demonstrate it to you? I try and I try, and you still insist on vexing my patience by dating and canoodling with other guys. Well, no more! It's time the world discovered who you really are! Once no one is clamoring over you trying to reveal your secret, I'll have you all to myself.
> Love you forever,
> Dan.

"The guy needs to go into a mental institution," Xena said.

"Your job, Prowler, is to find and stop him." Jessica flung her arm over her eyes. "If he reveals my true species, my life will be over!"

Xena rolled her eyes. "That's bit dramatic, Jessica, don't you think?"

Jessica peeked out from under her arm to sneer at Xena. "You have no idea what my species' culture is like."

"Well . . . then what is your species?"

"None of your business."

"She a peacock," Hunter said, still studying the letters.

"I am *not* a peacock!" Jessica hopped to her feet, her body feathers bristling. "I am a peahen!"

Xena blinked. "A . . . peahen?"

"Yes, a peahen, the proper name for a female peafowl." Jessica snorted. "Honestly, people in this world are so ignorant. They don't know the proper names of anything—"

"Actually." Xena raised a finger. "I know what a peahen is. I was just surprised that you're one of them. Peahens are so . . ." She trailed off.

"Drab? Boring? Unappealing? One-note?" Jessica crossed her arms.

"Well . . . yeah."

"And you would be right." Jessica fell silent a moment, her three crest feathers drooping. "In peafowl society, peahens are supposed to be demure, silent, and still . . . the total opposite of me. I love color and music and dancing and flamboyant dresses! But I don't want to give up my peafowl culture. My family is high society . . . lots of parties with the rich and powerful. It's wondrous. But my behavior on stage is scandalous. Never mind that if I was a peacock, it would be no problem." She sighed. "In any case, my parents relented to me being a singer if I kept my identity a secret. If anyone found out who I was, they'd disown me—the scandal would be too great. I'd still have my fans and my career, but . . . I want it all!"

"So that's why you dress like this." Xena motioned to Jessica's costume.

"Exactly. How'd you figure it out, Prowler?" Jessica turned her nose up at him. "I've been very careful, and no one else has ever done it before."

"It my job, chickie." Hunter tossed the letters into his bag. "I dids research."

"What sort of research?" Jessica crossed her arms. "I want to know so I can squash it."

"Come on, Hun—uh, Prowler." Xena tilted her head at him. "Tell us."

"Fine." Hunter snorted his nose then swallowed. "Two things: One . . ." He placed three fingers on top of his head.

"My crest?" Jessica ran her hands over her head.

"Look like a peacock."

"Peahen," Jessica said.

"But that doesn't mean anything." Xena gazed at Jessica's feathers. "She's had all sorts of crests over the years. Once, she had one like a cockatiel. That was cool."

"But she alway has a crest." Hunter pressed his fingers together. "Im-gens only disguise. They dun fake sum'tin that's not there." He pointed at Jessica. "Her specie got a crest."

"So what?" Jessica turned up her beak. "Lots of birds have crests."

"Which bring me to two." Hunter tapped his nose.

"My beak?" Jessica crossed her eyes to look at hers.

"Again she's had several beaks over the years." Xena clasped her hands. "My favorite was the one that looked like a chickadee. It was so cute."

"I know, right." Jessica grinned at her.

"But dis de Isle." Hunter gave a nasty grin. "No im-gens allowed. There's not'in to hide that peacock schnoze."

"Pea*hen*!" Jessica stomped her foot on the carpet. "I am a peahen!"

"Ignore him." Xena waved his hand at Hunter. "He's messing with you now."

"Don't forget you signed a non-disclosure agreement." Jessica poked Hunter's chest. "If you or her tell anyone about this, I'll sue you for everything you have and ship you right off to jail."

Hunter pressed his lips together. His eyes narrowed at her.

"Can she do that?" Xena looked in Hunter's eyes. "Send you to jail if we tell?"

"In my case, yes. But dun worry, Babe. Squealin' to the press ain't my style."

"Well." Jessica stood straight. "Since you know my secret, do you mind if I take off this costume?" She didn't wait for an answer. She twisted and pulled her tail until it popped off, revealing short, brown tail feathers. "This thing weighs about 30 pounds." She held up her tail-extensions.

"Wow." Xena gazed at Jessica as she pulled off her feathery wig. Underneath was a stocking cap holding down her long, brown hair-feathers.

"This wig is so hot!" Jessica shook out her "hair."

Xena stared at the contrast of brown feathers of her hair verses yellow feathers on her face and arms. "So . . . how do you keep your body feathers yellow?"

"Semi-permanent feather dye." Jessica pulled the gloves off of her hands. "This will wash out in 10 more showers or so. But my new costumes will be arriving from the GFG Corporation soon—you know, the bioelectrical giant that developed the SF Emulator?"

"The GFG Corporation . . . I know them." Xena felt her electricity flare. She had been held prisoner there about two years ago and ruthlessly experimented on to find out the secret of her fur. Their experiments allowed them to develop the technology Jessica was gushing about.

"My new costume will be totally bio-electrically controlled. All I'll have to do is think it, and it'll respond like real feathers." Jessica clasped her hands. "It'll be so realistic, no one will be able to tell the difference. The gap between real and costume will close even further."

"And now I's bored." Hunter hefted himself out of the chair. "Time to go, Zed."

"Oh, okay." Xena waved at Jessica. "Nice to meet you, Jessica. And don't worry. We'll find out who Dan is."

"Thank you." Jessica nodded at her. "And one more thing, Prowler."

Hunter paused at the door.

"Don't let anyone know you're working for me." Jessica sneered at him. "I have a reputation."

"I won't." Hunter raised the corner of his lip. "I gots a rep azzel."

"Azzel?" Xena walked out the door, repeating that word to herself. It wasn't until Hunter closed the door behind her that she realized he meant, "as well."

"So? What'd you think?" Hunter's voice and manner returned to normal as soon as he was out in the hallway.

"What do I think?" Xena hopped down the hallway to the elevator. "I met Jessica! I think I'm going to be the envy of all my friends."

"Was it worth giving up our date over?" Hunter slipped his arm around her.

"Yeah, but . . ." Xena crossed her arms. "Why didn't you tell her I was your girlfriend? Apprentice, indeed!"

Hunter scratched one of his ears. "That was an oversight on my part. I was so excited to have you meet her that I overlooked the obvious. I don't want anyone to know what I do or who I am, and I don't want them to come after you because of me."

"What you do . . . are you really a bounty hunter?"

"Didn't you know?"

Xena shook her head.

Hunter shrugged. "Thought it was obvious after the Expermian thing."

"Does Daddy know? He doesn't like bounty hunters, for obvious reasons."

"Do you think he would let me keep hanging around you if he didn't know everything about me?" Hunter stopped at the elevator. "He's like living background check."

"That's good. I wouldn't want him to beat your face in—at least not before you take me to that concert."

"Nice to know that's all you care about." Hunter chuckled.

"I can't wait to see her sing in person." Xena hopped onto the elevator when it opened. "I've never been to a concert."

"I'm glad you're excited about it." Hunter stepped beside her on the elevator. "I had to convince her I needed two passes instead of one as part of the job. I didn't think I'd pull it off."

"Wait. What?" Xena swung around to face him. "Is that how you were able to get them? Because it's a part of your job?"

Hunter winced. "Yeah, but . . . that's the only way I could get you there."

"So when we go, it won't really be a date." Xena's ears fell. "You'll be working . . . again."

"Xena, come on . . ."

"Forget it." Xena crossed her arms.

Hunter smacked his forehead. Then his ears pricked up. "Listen, Z, if I can get this job done before the concert, we can go together so . . ."

"So you're going to work non-stop on it now to finish in time?"

"It's the only way." Hunter looked at Xena with wide eyes.

Xena inhaled through her nose. "Fine. But I'm going to help you."

"You?"

"I'm your apprentice, aren't I?"

"And a lovely apprentice you are." Hunter kissed her cheek.

Xena had to concentrate to keep her electricity from shooting out and shorting the elevator. The last thing she wanted was to be stuck on an elevator with Hunter because if that happened, he'd never get his work done. And she'd never make it to that concert.

CHAPTER 4

"Are they gone?" Alex peeked into the parlor with a coffee cup in one hand.

"Yeah." Jessica plopped on the chair.

"Latte." Alex handed it to her. "I don't think it was wise to let those two in on our problem. I had it sorted."

"I'm not the type to sit back and let things happen. I'd rather do something." Jessica sipped the latte. She balked. "This is disgusting. Can't you make a decent latte?" She set it on the table beside her.

Alex said nothing. He was used to her diva fits, though this one seemed more subdued than normal. "What happened to your wig and tail?"

"Took it off." Jessica rested her cheek in her hands. "By the way, wasn't my new costume supposed to be delivered by the time I got here?"

Alex inhaled through his teeth. "There's a slight problem. The bulk of the costume was delivered, but the mesh that enables the bioelectrical component is backordered. It's . . . not here yet."

"What?" Jessica shot to her feet. "How am I supposed to use the costume without it? It weighs, like, 60 pounds!"

"The military gets priority, and they needed the available mesh for the Expermian War." Alex held up his hands. "But don't get excited, I called the company, and they are making a special order for you. You will have it here before the concert." He rubbed the back of his head. ". . . but you won't have time to practice with it."

"Unacceptable, Alex!" Jessica snatched the latte and splashed it in his face.

Alex clamped his eyes shut as warm coffee slapped his face. Good thing he had anticipated this and had not made it as hot as Jessica liked it.

"You are so useless!" Jessica snatched her wig off the chair. "Taylor! Get me back in this thing. I'm going out!"

"Where are you going?" Alex wiped coffee from his eyes.

"None of your business!" Jessica poked his chest. "All you have to worry about is getting my entire costume here before my dress rehearsal. Taylor!"

"Here!" Taylor appeared with a make-up kit like a toolbox in hand.

"On second thought, I don't want to get back in my full costume." Jessica tossed the wig aside. "Dye my feathers yellow so I can go out." She marched toward the bathroom.

"Yes, ma'am." Taylor scurried after her.

"And make it quick." Jessica snapped her fingers.

"Yes, ma'am." Taylor slipped into the bathroom before Jessica slammed the door so hard the portraits on the wall rattled.

Alex sighed. Now that was the sort of diva tantrum he was used to.

CHAPTER 5

"A peahen. She's a peahen." Xena sat on the black couch in the family room in the house she and her family were staying in. The house had an open concept design—every room flowing one into the other without walls to separate them. The windows and sliding door leading to the backyard were open to let in the sun and the cool, ocean breeze that fluttered the white, lacy curtains.

Xena rested her cheek on her hands. "There's such a disconnect there."

"Probably because all the peahens you know are prim and proper like she said." Hunter sat on the floor in front of the couch. He had connected his computer to the TV to get a better view of the pictures he scrolled through.

"I guess." Xena tapped her fingers against her cheek. "It's hard for me to picture a peahen being so . . . gaudy."

"But peacocks sure are allowed to be." Kathra, Xena's little sister, came down the stairs. Her blonde hair was pulled back in a braid, and her white fur had been tinted yellow by the afternoon sun. "I don't think it's fair. Peahens should be able to do anything they want. But I can't judge another species' culture unless I have lived among them and studied it in depth." She rested her arms on the back of the couch beside Xena's head. "So why are we talking about peafowl anthropology?"

"*We* were." Hunter pointed to Xena and himself. "You inserted yourself into our conversation."

Kathra blew a raspberry at him. "So why, *Xena*?"

"Um . . . because . . ." Xena's ears fell. What could she say that wouldn't give away Jessica's secret?

"We met a peahen today, and Xena was shocked at her behavior." Hunter swiped the screen again. He didn't even miss a beat.

"That's right." Xena nodded at Kathra. "She was out there and loud and vain."

"I see." Kathra's turned her blue eyes to the ceiling. "Yeah . . . I'd be confused too if I met someone like that, but is it because of peafowl culture or our prejudices, I wonder."

"No idea." Xena shook her head. At 12 years old, Kathra was one of the smartest people Xena knew. A genius, probably.

"So what are you looking at?" Kathra turned her attention to the screen. "Pictures of Jessica's concert? I didn't know you were a fan, Hunter?"

Hunter flattened his ears. "I'm not."

"Hunter got a job helping Jessica. He has to find and expose a crazed fan who's threatening to expose her secret." Xena turned to her sister. "It's crazy. The guy broke into her house while she was sleeping."

"Oh, wow!" Kathra's eyes grew wide.

"That's why Hunter is looking at those pictures." Xena flattened one of her ears. "Not sure how this will help him, though."

"The way I figure it, 'Dan' has to be someone in Jessica's entourage." Hunter's eyes didn't leave the television screen. "It has to be someone who would have unrestricted access to her. I was hoping to get a clue by comparing the incidents described in the letters with pictures of her and her concerts, but . . . everyone in her entourage is accounted for when Dan sneaks into her stuff."

"Maybe that guy is working with someone in her staff." Kathra flipped herself over the back of the couch and landed in a heap beside Xena. "If one of them gave him access to Jessica's stuff . . ."

"That's theory number two." Hunter held up two fingers.

"But why would anyone who works with Jessica want to do that?" Xena said.

Kathra shrugged. "Publicity stunt?"

"And not tell Jessica about it?" Xena said.

Kathra shrugged again.

"This is a shot of an incident at her concert two months ago." Hunter pointed to the television screen. "Someone managed to slip in an im-gen jammer into her costume. What the world didn't know at the time was that most of Jessica's costume is a physical disguise, so no one noticed anything. However, those jammers' remotes don't have a long range."

"Which means the guy might be in this picture." Xena pointed at the screen.

"He must be in this area right here." Hunter tapped on his computer, and a circle appeared on the screen. It zoomed in on an area including the front row and a bit of back stage. "Any further, and he wouldn't be within range of Jessica on stage to set it off."

"It's him." Kathra tapped the screen on a brown, spotted, weasel-looking animal with a striped tail. "That civet right there at the edge of the crowd."

Hunter chuckled. "You can't just guess, Kat."

"I don't guess." Kathra crossed her arm and snorted.

"Why do you think it's him?" Xena asked.

"Because he's the only one in the circle wearing a full image-generator." Kathra thrust her nose in the air. "That's the easiest way to disguise yourself."

"But if he set off an im-gen jammer when he's wearing one himself, he might be exposed too," Xena said.

"And so would all the other fans wearing image-generators." Kathra raised her chin. "He'd look like part of the crowd that was affected by it—collateral damage. Besides, everyone would be looking at Jessica, so no one would care about him."

"Th-that's . . ." Hunter gazed at Kathra. "And how do you even know he's wearing a full image-generator?"

Kathra gave a triumphant grin. "Daddy and I have been researching image-generators and how they work—so he can tweak one that will never short out for Xena. Image-generators rearrange light patterns so that the eye takes in whatever the it presents, but it can't fool cameras. When an image is recorded, there's a slight haze around the wearer."

Xena peered at the screen. Sure enough, the culprit had a blur around him.

"You're right." Hunter's mouth dropped open. "I never noticed that before."

"Other people are starting to spot it, too." Kathra flipped her braid. "Daddy says that the next generation of im-gens don't have this problem, but when they come out you'll have to get a permit to wear one like you do for a full image-generator."

"You need a permit to wear a full image-generator?" Xena looked from Hunter to Kathra. "Even when you're off the Isle?"

"Otherwise, people would be committing crimes, and the police wouldn't know who to look for." Hunter tapped on his computer. "Of course, some people get them without permits anyway, but that's the nature of things."

"Hey! Hunter." Kathra bounced on the seat. "Maybe you can try looking for a permit for this guy."

"I thought of that, but first I have to find out who he is." Hunter smacked the 'enter' key. "By enhancing and removing the interference caused by the image-generator, we can see his true self." As he spoke, the picture pixelated and reloaded, revealing a skunk. "That's our guy. Let's see if we can find a match . . ."

"Xena!" The front door burst open, and Mira's voice sailed in. "You are going to love me!"

"Hi, Mira!" Xena waved over the couch. "We're in here." She took a second to check that her image-generator was working before Mira rushed in, holding a shopping bag.

"Xena, wait until I tell you what I did—" Mira froze. "Oh, honey, you have some terrible static cling."

"Huh?"

Mira lifted Xena's arm.

A pen and a sheet of paper had stuck fast to Xena's elbow. "Not again." She shook her arm, then pulled the paper off. It stuck to her hand. "Oh, no."

"Don't worry about it." Mira pulled a sheet of cloth out of her purse. "I got some stuff at home that will take care of it. You rub it on your fur after a shower, and no more static cling. It's fabulous! In the meantime, have a fabric sheet. I keep them on me just in case."

"Thanks." Xena rubbed the sheet on her fur. The pen and paper dropped to the floor.

Hunter collected them. "Have you been working on your exercises to control your field?" he whispered to her.

Xena glanced at Mira and whispered, "Non-stop."

"We're going to have to work harder at it, then," Hunter said.

"Whoa!" Mira looked at the picture on the screen. "Way too much make-up for you, skunkie. Anyway, back to important matters. Guess what I did. You are going to love me."

"I give up. What did you do?" Xena crumpled the dryer sheet in her hands.

"Jessica is having a party tonight, and I got your name on the guest list."

"Really?" Xena jumped up and caught Mira's hands. "Mira, you're amazing!"

"I know!" Mira sang. "I felt so bad that I couldn't get you tickets to the concert, so I got Mama to add your name to the list before she approved the party. You too, Hunter—maybe you can escort Xena . . . spend some quality time with her." She winked at Xena. "And you two can meet my new boyfriend."

"What about me?" Kathra bounced on the couch. "Did Aunt Chloe add my name to the list."

"Sorry, Kat." Mira shook her head. "Jessica's parties are not quite age appropriate for you . . . or so Mama says."

"Aw." Kathra flung herself back in the couch.

"It's okay, Kathra." Xena sat on the couch beside her. "I wouldn't want to go to a party without Hunter, and he's gotta work, so—"

"Oh, I'll go." Hunter shut down his computer. "I have to do something to thank you for being a good sport all day."

"Really?" Xena's ears pricked. Then they lowered. "But then . . . what about Kathra . . ."

"It's okay, Xena." Kathra gave her a huge smile. "Go and have a good time."

"You don't mind?" Xena took her hands. "Are you sure?"

Kathra clasped her hands tight. "As long as you let me dress you up."

Xena's ears dropped. "Oh, wait. No, no . . ."

"Oh, yes!" Mira grabbed Xena's arm. "Let's go! Time to get you in something presentable." She raised the bag in her hand. "I came prepared!"

"I'm going to wash up and change." Hunter side-stepped them and headed to the front door. "I'll be back to pick you up, Zizzie."

"Careful." Mira called as she pulled Xena upstairs. "You may not recognize her when you get back."

"I'm okay with that." Hunter waved over his shoulder.

"You are not funny, Hunter." Xena shouted

Hunter winked at her before he walked out, shutting the door behind him.

CHAPTER 6

Xena glowered at the pebbly road. "That beast, Mira. She slapped on these stupid clothes on me and then took off."

Mira had dressed her in a lavender top and had tied a black, satin ribbon around her waist. Her skirt was made up of three layers of fabric, one layer reaching further down her legs than the one above it. The top layer was made up of dark purple chiffon, the next of black chiffon, and the last was made up of lavender dyed cotton. Her hair was tied back in a ribbon.

"I don't look right in any of this stuff." Xena held her purple purse in the air. "And this thing is useless."

Hunter had his eyes glued to his phone. "Then why do you have it?"

"Kathra says it pulls the look together."

"I don't know why you get upset when you dress up." Hunter caught her hand. "You look great."

"Thanks."

The club where Jessica's party was being held was a half a mile from Xena's home so they decided to walk. The sun had faded from the sky, and the stars had not yet appeared. The heat of the day had started to ebb.

Xena gazed at the road in the twilight. Ocean waves roared like trees in a summer gale, and the sand had turned a grayish-purple hue in the fading light. If it hadn't been for the mosquitoes landing on her fur being zapped by her electricity, causing small sparks all over her arms, Xena would have thought it was romantic.

She took a deep breath and tried to keep her electricity in check. Nothing like ruining a romantic moment by zapping your boyfriend. She glowered at him. Or by paying more attention to your phone than to your girlfriend. "Hunter, what are you looking at?"

"Finishing up some stuff for the Jessica assignment." Hunter tapped his phone. "I got a notification right before I left to pick you up. Kathra was right. Dan did have a permit for a full image-generator. This is him." He held his phone out to her.

Xena bit back a comment about him working . . . again . . . and looked at the phone. On it was a profile picture of a skunk. He had the usual black and white fur, and a bright smile that made Xena want to get to know him. His light brown eyes contrasted nicely with the dark fur around his eyes. "Christopher Cutter," she read.

"And get this: I did some research, and his middle name is Daniel." Hunter shook his head. "The criminals I come across in my line of work aren't geniuses, that's for sure." He swiped at his phone. "But I can't wrap my head around this guy. He's a professional photographer, but he doesn't seem like the sort who'd go off the deep-end."

"Are they ever 'that sort'?"

"Nah, but I can usually find something that raises a red flag, but with him . . . nothing." Hunter studied his phone for a little while longer before he slipped it in his pocket. "Ah, well. Psychoanalyzing him is not my job, and knowing who he is solves a lot of questions. I'm willing to guess he's been one of the photographers hired to shoot Jessica's concerts, which means he'd be able to get close to her without raising alarms."

"So I guess your theory of someone in Jessica's entourage being behind this wasn't correct, after all."

Hunter shrugged. "It happens. I'll get my info on him together and head off the Isle tomorrow to catch him. Then I'll be free as a bird."

"Off the Isle?"

"Not likely he'd be here, Z." Hunter stretched. "Chloe runs a tight ship. This island is more secure than the Drymairadian palace. No one can break in here." He cracked his neck. "I wonder what I'll do when I get back," he muttered to himself. "Maybe I'll go back to school. I'd have to do a few jobs to afford it, though . . ."

"What are you talking about?"

"Oh, um . . ." Hunter averted his eyes. "I'm retiring . . . well, not entirely. I've got to do enough to eat, but I'm hanging up the H Prowler name."

"Why? I thought you liked your job." Xena pressed her lips together. "You sure are obsessed with it lately."

"I do, but I . . ." Hunter trailed off with a shrug.

"You're not going to tell me?"

"It's not worth talking about." Hunter squeezed her hands. "I'd rather talk about you. After this job is done, nothing will come between us."

Xena's heart jumped. She had to turn away from Hunter before he saw her face flush beet red.

A haze of light illuminated the road ahead. Music boomed through the air, and spotlight shone on a building labelled, "Club Bando," by a sign above the door.

Xena pointed. "That must be it."

"So it is," Hunter led her to the front of the club.

A pelican stood at the door, his wings folded. "Name."

"Xena." She pointed at the clipboard. "I should be on the list."

"So should I," Hunter tapped the list. "Name's Hunter."

The bouncer gave a squawk close to a grunt and stepped aside to let them in.

The house lights were off, and colored spotlights lights flashed over a dance floor crowded with revelers. At one end was a counter where teenagers and young adults of all species sat on stools drinking colored drinks that the otter behind the counter served them. Behind the otter, glasses and bottles glittered in the strobe lights. Inside of those bottles were liquids ranging in color from brown to green to blue, all shining in the dimness. The music blasted so loud, it was a wonder the drink bottles didn't shatter to the floor.

"It's a bar!" Xena exclaimed.

"Haven't you ever been in a club?" Hunter shouted to be heard over the pounding music. "It's a glorified bar with a dance floor. I doubt they're serving alcohol tonight, though. Underage drinking is something that Chloe would frown upon."

Xena swung her purse around a few times. "So . . . what do we do now?"

Hunter stared at her a moment. "Wow, Xena. I need to take you out more." He took her hand and led her to the dance floor.

"Why is it that we always end up dancing together?" Xena said, trying to sway in time with the music.

"I don't know." Hunter gyrated his hips. "We must like it." He crinkled his nose at her.

Xena glanced around at the crowd. Everyone was dancing, talking, laughing with huge grins on their faces. "Jessica knows how to throw a party."

"Speaking of, there she is," Hunter pointed.

Xena turned to the direction Hunter pointed. Jessica, back in costume, hopped like a kangaroo and screamed at the top of her lungs. She had a soda in her hand and was surrounded by a crowd of boys.

"She looks like she's having the best time of all," Hunter said.

"I hope that drink's not spiked," Xena said.

Hunter watched Jessica a few seconds more. "If we weren't on the Isle, I'd wonder if one of them wasn't her stalker," he muttered.

Xena halted. "Are you thinking about your job?"

"No! Of course not!" Hunter's ears fell. "I was making an observation."

Xena clenched her fists. Her face reddened and then . . . she sighed. "I don't know why I even try. I'm getting something to drink." She retreated to the drink bar. "One cherry soda, please."

The bartender filled a tall glass and handed it to her. "Five dollars."

"Shoot!" Xena patted her skirt. "I didn't think to bring any money."

Hunter slid a bill to the bartender before sitting on the stool beside Xena.

Xena took the drink and turned her back to him.

"You have every right to be mad at me, Xena." Hunter ran his hands through his hair. "This job has saturated my mind . . . and my life . . . non-stop. Please be patient with me. It's vital that I finish this."

"And that's more important than me, I guess," Xena muttered.

"What did you say?"

Xena shook her head. "Nothing." Her eyes fell on her legs— her thin, spindly legs. She tugged her skirt down as far as it could go and wished that Mira had put her in pants instead. She loathed her legs; she despised the way they looked in the skirt—like two toothpicks poking out of a napkin.

Maybe Shandra was right. Maybe Hunter neglected her because he was bored . . . or maybe fed up. After all, her life never stayed stable for long. In her fifteen years, she'd been kidnapped, experimented on, ostracized, forced out of her home, had ran away, been nearly worshipped and idolized, and manipulated as a power source for a weapon of mass destruction.

But all that might have been tolerable if Xena had been something to look at. But she wasn't. Plain faced with a stick, straight figure, she never looked right in anything she wore. Not like all the other girls on the dancefloor with their curves, clothes, and hair. Even the guys looked better in their clothes than she did in hers. She groaned. Why did fashion have to be such a major concern, anyway? And why did she have to hide out on the Isle de Losierres, the fashion capital of the world? This island . . . this party . . . belonged to the beautiful people, not the plain Xenas of the world. She and her plain looks must have stuck out like a sore thumb. Just like the black and white tuxedo cat over in the corner.

Xena did a double-take. The cat was dressed in black from head to toe, and a hood covered his face. "That's weird."

"What is?"

"That cat over there." Xena didn't take his eyes off of him, though keeping track of him standing in the dark was tricky. "He's wearing a black hoodie and black jeans. It's . . . not something anyone on the Isle would wear to a party like this, is it?"

Hunter's eyes narrowed as he studied the cat. "That's not a cat."

"It's not?" Xena kept her eyes on him. He fiddled with something in the pocket of his hoodie. His eyes stared straight at one point in the center of the room. Xena followed his gaze and saw his target: Jessica. "That doesn't look good."

"Oh, crap!" Hunter hopped off of the stool and slid into the crowd faster than Xena could have imagined. He took a flying leap over the ocean of guys and shouted, "I love you, Jessica!" He landed on her, tackling her to the ground. The crowd scattered.

Something whizzed by the air where she had been. It gleamed in the light before it disappeared in the hall leading to the bathrooms.

"What are you doing, you freak?" Jessica screeched.

The music halted. The house lights came up. Everyone stopped to stare at Hunter and Jessica.

"I . . . am your biggest fan." Hunter gave her an unconvincing grin.

"Get off!" Jessica shoved him off. She hopped to her feet. Her beak ground together. "Drift!" The wolverine appeared at her side. "Throw him out!"

"Hey, wait a minute!" Hunter tried to run, but Drift caught him under his arms and lifted him to the door. The crowd parted at his approach. "You don't understand." Hunter kicked his feet. "Hold up!"

Drift carried him to the door and tossed him outside.

Xena hopped off her seat to run after Hunter but hesitated. That thing that whizzed by Jessica . . . what was it? That cat . . . or whatever he was . . . had been trying to hit her. Xena scanned the crowd for him. He had disappeared in the chaos.

The music resumed and the light dimmed again. Xena darted in the direction the thing had flown. If she was that cat and had failed to do whatever he was planning, the first thing she would do was to try and retrieve that thing before anyone else found it.

She reached the bathroom hallway and scanned the floor. Not many people were here so Xena was relatively undisturbed in her search. Something gleamed in the corner, catching her eye. A plastic dart, painted dull silver with gray feathers glued to the end, had stuck onto the baseboard. Xena reached down to get it, but halted, remembering the crime dramas she'd watched on TV. You don't want to leave your fingerprints on the evidence. She reached in her purse to get one of the dryer sheets that Mira left in there for her and tugged on the dart. She had expected it to pop right off, but the rubber stopper held fast. She yanked it until it pulled free. To her surprise, a tiny needle had been set into the rubber.

Someone hissed. Xena swung around. The cat loomed behind her, staring at her with bright, green eyes.

"Give it here." He extended a black furred hand. It had no claws that she could see and no white patches on the fingers like other tuxedo cats she'd known.

Xena felt electricity flare off of her fur. She pulled it back in to make sure she didn't electrocute anyone by accident, dropped the dart in her purse, and raised her fists in front of her face. "Come get it." She crouched in a defensive posture.

The cat, if that was what it was, took a step back before racing at her. Xena side-stepped him and struck the back of his neck with her elbow. He sprawled on the ground, but flipped over onto his feet. He glared at her with fierce eyes and tail—a rather fluffy tail for a cat—bristling. A white stripe ran down it.

"Dan!" Xena clenched her teeth.

"Xena!" Mira's voice rang out over the music. "Xena, there you are."

The cat hissed again and darted into the bathroom.

Mira rushed over to her towing a gray chinchilla. "Xena, I have been looking for you everywhere. Where is your phone?"

Xena glanced at Mira before looking toward the bathroom for Dan. "I left it at home, I think."

Mira sighed in exasperation. "I will never understand you. Anyway, I want you to meet Morrin." She wrapped her arms around his.

"I'm sorry, Mira, but—" Xena turned to them. "Hey, it's you!"

Morrin tail straightened. "No way. You're . . ." He snapped his fingers. "You're Hunter's girl. What's your name again?"

"Xena."

"That's it." Morrin looked her up and down. "Gotta say, you look more the part this time around."

"Do you two know each other?" Mira hung on to his arm.

"He's Hunter's friend." Xena held her hands behind her back. "I met him when Hunter and I went on our first date."

"That was your first date?" Morrin whistled. "How'd you get your hooks in him so fast?"

Xena's ears pricked. "Excuse me?"

"Morrin, would you go get me a drink please, sweetie?" Mira rubbed her nose on his cheek.

"Of course." Morrin returned the gesture.

Xena balked as Mira watched him head to the bar.

"Oh dang, he's so hot. Doesn't have much of a filter, though." Mira bit her index finger as she watched him. After a moment, she turned to Xena. "So what's the deal with Hunter? Why did he tackle Jessica like that?"

"Long story. I have to find him." Xena pushed her way through the crowd and dashed out the front door where Hunter stood cursing at the bouncer.

"You have to let me back in!" Hunter tried to shove past him.

"No bothering the stars." The pelican shoved him to the

ground. "Ever!"

"Hunter!" Xena rushed to his side.

"That's enough, Dalton." Mira emerged behind her. "Good work."

"Yes, Miss Mira." Dalton crossed his arms and blocked the door.

"Mira." Hunter scrambled to his feet. "Mira, you have to let me back in there."

"Why?"

"It's a job." Hunter danced on his toes. "Come on. Time's running out."

Mira pressed her lips together, then nodded. She turned to Dalton. "Let him in."

"But—"

"It's okay." Mira smiled at him. "I'll explain it to Mama later."

Dalton squawk-grunted and stepped aside.

"But Hunter." Mira pointed at him. "Make sure Jessica doesn't see you."

"Gotcha."

"Oh, Hunter, wait." Xena caught his arm before he went inside. "I saw him. I saw Dan. He tried to fight me but then ran off to the bathroom. I didn't see him come out, though."

Hunter paused for a moment. "He probably jumped out a window." He started off but skidded to a halt. "I'm sorry, Xena, but—"

"No, no, no. Go." Xena waved him off. "This is serious."

"I owe you." Hunter kissed her cheek before darting around the building.

"Want to tell me what's going on?" Mira put a hand on her hip.

"A crazed fan is trying to expose Jessica." Xena watched where Hunter disappeared. "He tried to shoot something at her at the party. That's why Hunter tackled her."

"Whoa, whoa, whoa." Mira waved her hands. "How did someone like that get on the Isle?"

"I don't know."

"Mama is not going to like this." Mira pulled out her phone. "I better tell her. What did he try to shoot her with?"

"This." Xena dug in her purse and pulled out the dart. "Oh, shoot! I didn't get a chance to tell Hunter about it."

"Looks like a toy." Mira flicked it with her fingernails.

"But look." Xena held it up so that Mira saw the needle.

Mira's brows furrowed. "What in the—what is it?"

"I don't know. And I couldn't begin to guess how anyone could use this to expose Jessica."

"The tip is wet."

"Oh, yeah?" Xena examined it. A bead of moisture had coalesced on the needle's edge. She pulled several tissues from her purse and wrapped the dart in it. If that liquid did anything bad to image-generators, she didn't want it to touch her.

"Good thing Hunter's on the job." Mira looked in the direction he had gone. "He's the best there is."

"You know what Hunter does?"

"Course. Didn't you?"

"Not till this afternoon."

"Oh." Mira fell quiet a moment. "Ew. Xena, what is that on your elbow?"

Xena turned her elbow to see a black smudge smeared on it. "I don't know."

Mira wiped her finger on it. "It's make-up—greasepaint. How'd you get this on you?"

"Dunno." Xena watched Mira pull out a make-up removing wipe from her purse. "I did hit Dan with my elbow, but that was on the back of his neck."

"Dan? Is that that guy you all were looking at in your house this afternoon?" Mira wiped the blotch off of Xena's elbow. "I told you he was wearing way too much make-up."

"But why would a skunk wear black greasepaint?"

"I have no idea what goes through the minds of the fashion-inept." Mira tossed the wipe back in her purse. "But like I said, don't worry about it. Hunter's the best. He'll catch the guy no matter what type of disguise he wears."

"Good to know."

Mira's phone buzzed. "That's Morrin. He's wondering where I am."

"I'm going to go and see if I can't figure out what this is." Xena placed the dart in her purse.

"Bye, Xena." Mira waved at her. "Keep me in the loop, okay?"

"You got it!" Xena trotted off down the road.

CHAPTER 7

"**D**id you figure out what that stuff in the dart is yet?" Xena leaned over the back of Kathra's chair.

"Don't rush me." Kathra shrugged Xena off and went back to examining her scanner.

Xena took to pacing again. The delay chafed at her. Kathra and J.R., their father, sat at the round table between the kitchen and the living room. Once Xena had returned home and revealed her find, J.R.'s ears had gone flat. As a notorious criminal wanted the world over, his mind hurtled toward the worst possible scenario, and he insisted they uncover its contents immediately. That meant Kathra had been called in. According to J.R., she was handier with a scanner than most professionals.

Kathra draped the table with some plastic and then a layer of flame-resistant, absorbent fabric. The floor underneath and around the table received the same treatment. They had gotten these items from the basement, but neither J.R. nor Kathra would tell Xena why they were down there. That done, Kathra had donned gloves, protective goggles, and a lab coat made of the same fabric they had spread on the table.

The dart had been filled with drops of liquid, and she had set one of these on a slide.

"This is hard." Kathra screwed her mouth up in a pout. "I didn't think analyzing unknown substances would be so difficult."

"That's because you ain't done it before." J.R. ruffled her hair. "Can't be an instant expert at everything, Kitten."

"Don't do that." Kathra moved her head from his reach.

Xena stopped in her pacing long enough to smile at her sister and her father. Compared to the big, hulking, muscle-bound mass of brown fur that was J.R., Kathra looked like a doll. J.R.'s sharp ears swiveled left and right—never stopping, always listening for a threat. It made her smile fade. He had been a fugitive for so long, he couldn't relax, not even on someplace as secure as the Isle. Of course, maybe the Isle wasn't so secure, if Dan had made it on.

"I don't think it's wise to do this on the dining table." Karalaina, their mother, glanced at them from the kitchen. In her hands she held a bowl of banana fritter batter she was testing for a catering recipe. She was a vixen like Xena and Kathra, being their birth mother, and her wavy, blonde hair fell over her shoulders as she bent over the table. Like Hunter, she was an Expermian fox, so her hair faded to a shade of auburn at the ends. Her ears were three times as large as Xena's. "If that stuff is dangerous it shouldn't be on the same surface that food is on."

J.R. stifled a growl, though Xena heard it rumble in his throat. "We put plastic on the table, didn't we?"

"And this fabric will absorb and contain anything that falls on it, so it's okay." Kathra kept her eyes on the scanner.

Karalaina shook her head and turned back to the burners. She moved with a grace that matched her perfect features—hour-glass figure; silky, salmon-colored fur; bright, pale blue eye—the complete opposite of Xena. She dropped batter in a hot pan, and in a few moments, Xena heard the sound of fritters frying. The scent of cinnamon, bananas, and caramelized sugar wafted through the air.

"First dibs on taste testing." Xena raised her hand. "If I like how it comes out, will you teach me how to make it, Mom?"

Karalaina paused, her ears standing straight up. Xena let her ears angle back. Karalaina was probably surprised. She hadn't been in their lives long, and Xena was still trying to get used to her—so she didn't ask Karalaina for much.

"Of course, sweetie." Karalaina smiled, her eyes wrinkling at the edges.

Xena plopped in a chair. Even her mother's crow's feet were beautiful.

"It did it again." Kathra pounded her fists on the table. "This same message pops up every time I try to analyze. It says it's 30% water, 23% various types of salt, and 47% of something that's, 'No known match.' But the water and salt content goes up every time, and the unknown keeps going down."

"No known match, huh?" J.R. fingered his chin. "That means that the database we're usin' don't have a chemical match."

"But I'm using the Drymairad Pharmaceutical, Medicinal, and Chemical Database." Kathra slumped in her chair. "There's no public database in the world that's better."

"Maybe we should get a lab to handle it, then," Xena said.

"Not worth the money." J.R. pinched his lips together. "If it's not in the DPMC database, no lab guys could find a match either."

"So no one knows what this is?" Xena gazed at the little dart.

J.R. stared at the dart for a moment. "We may have to hack into the government's private database," he muttered. Xena let her ears fall back. She didn't want Kathra to be involved in anything illegal. There had to be another way . . .

"Hmmm . . . I wonder . . ." Kathra tapped the buttons on her scanner. "I'll get a look at the chemical structure of this thing. If I can get a close match to a known substance, I can guess the sort of characteristics it has."

"Good idea, Kitten." J.R. ruffled her hair again.

"I said, stop!" Kathra smacked his hand away.

"It's a great idea." Xena nodded in agreement. Might as well pretend she knew what they were talking about.

The front door opened. "Xena, you home?" Hunter called.

"In the kitchen."

"We need to start locking that door," J.R. muttered.

"Did you find him?" Xena stood when Hunter walked in.

"Nah. He was long gone by the time I picked up his trail." Hunter kissed her cheek before glancing at the contents of the table. "What's going on here?"

"Kathra's analyzing the dart I found." Xena resumed her seat.

"What dart?"

"The one Dan shot at Jessica."

Hunter examined everything again. "He . . . shot a dart at Jessica? And you picked it up? That was dangerous, Z."

"I was just trying to help." Xena shrugged. "I thought it was some sort of image-generator disrupting thing."

"That's what I'm talking about." Hunter rubbed the fur on her shoulder. "What if it was? You'd be exposed."

"Apparently, it could be something even worse." Karalaina turned up her nose as she set another batch of fritters in the pan. "So of course they decide to analyze it on the kitchen table."

J.R. growled. "Can it, woman."

Hunter chuckled.

"Hey, I know this substance!" Kathra shot up from the table. "No one touch anything." She darted up the stairs.

Hunter bent over the contents of the table to take a closer look. "That dart . . . plastic. Easily hidden; no scanner would pick it up."

"Just the thing that could make it on the Isle." J.R. leaned back in his chair. "Chloe's not searching for lo-tech."

"But the question is, how did Dan get on the Isle?" Hunter fingered his whiskers.

Kathra clattered down the stairs with a book as big as her head in her hands. She set it on the floor and flipped through the pages. Xena glanced at the contents as she flipped; no pictures—or rather, no pictures that made sense to her. All she saw was diagrams of molecules and pictures of body parts riddled with sores and exposed bones. She had to turn away. "Couldn't you use the digital version of this book?"

"It's easier for me to find things when I'm flipping through pages than when I'm swiping a screen. Here it is!" Kathra stopped on a page. "Just as I thought. This stuff is deadly."

"Deadly?" Xena jerked her hands away from the table.

J.R. shoved his chair away.

"It's the same kind of neurotoxin that the snake people of the Gordonian Desert use to hunt their food—except this is very concentrated." Kathra ran her fingers across lines of text. "It's made by their bodies and comes out in their fangs. They have to milk themselves and put it in darts like these in order to hunt. So cool! But . . . I don't understand how it got here. Drymairad doesn't use this substance. It's not even allowed in the country."

"Someone who's travelled the world and has massive connections could do it . . ." Hunter bit his bottom lip.

"How do you know all that, Kat?" Xena let one of her ears flatten. "You said no one knows what it is."

"Just because the public doesn't know, doesn't mean no one can find out." Kathra thrust her nose in the air.

"If it's banned from import, chances are the government knows what it is but ain't tellin anyone else 'bout it." J.R. sniffed. "With good reason."

"According to this, that dart contains enough neurotoxin to kill five people of Jessica's approximate weight." Kathra looked up, her eyes wide. "That guy wanted Jessica dead . . . and quick."

J.R. gazed at the table. "We're gon to have to throw out this table."

"I told you," Karalaina sang from the kitchen.

"We don't have to." Kathra shut her book. "The stuff degrades quickly when it hits the air. By now, any of the toxin that has been exposed is salt and water. And I don't see the stuff in the dart lasting for more than a few days. That's probably why Dan used it in the first place. After it degrades, no one would be able to trace it."

"But this doesn't make sense." Xena threw her hands up. "Dan wants to expose Jessica, not kill her. He's a fan."

"I've been reading about this in some psychology books," Kathra said. "A fan can get so enamored by the star that they get obsessed to the point they can't stand sharing them with anyone else."

"But he didn't want to hurt her," Xena said. "Nothing in his letters indicated that."

"Something's not adding up." Hunter rapped his knuckles on his forehead. "I think that vain, little peacock is hiding something."

"That's a little speciest, don't you think, Hunter?" Karalaina said over her shoulder.

"Besides, she's a peahen, remember?" Xena said.

Kathra gasped. "She *is*?"

Hunter smirked. "Xena, you weren't supposed to tell."

"Huh? I didn't say anything. You did."

"I just used that expression . . . you know, 'vain as a peacock'?" Hunter grinned at her. "It was supposed to be an inside joke."

Xena's ears fell. "But . . ."

"So it's *true*?" Kathra bounced on her toes.

"You all can't tell anyone I told you." Xena placed her finger on her lips. "If you do, Hunter could go to jail."

"Hunter ain't going to jail for that." J.R. snorted through his nose. "Unfortunately."

"In my case, I could." Hunter took a deep breath. "I need more information on this job, but . . . hey!" He grinned at J.R. "Feel like doing a job with me tonight, J.R.?"

J.R. raised an eyebrow. "Eh?"

"I'm not so good at breaking and entering." Hunter shrugged. "When I break in, I'm trying to catch someone so it doesn't matter if they hear me or not. But I need to get to the bottom of this. If they catch me snooping, Dan might know I'm on to him. So will you help me?"

"Why should I?" J.R. bared his teeth. "I dun like you."

Hunter scratched his hair. "Because you'll be doing something good—"

"Is breaking and entering ever good?" Karalaina set some fritter on the breakfast bar. "Someone needs to strip the table to I can scrub it down. I don't care if that stuff degrades or not."

"I'm on it." J.R. gathered the plastic so that the dart and its contents were inside.

"Come on, J.R. Work with me." Hunter grabbed a napkin and rescued the dart. He sealed it in a zip-top bag, dropped that in another, and put the whole thing in another. "Don't you like this kind of thing?"

"What's it to you what I like or not?" J.R. stuffed the plastic into heavy duty garbage bags and triple bagged it like Hunter had done with the dart.

"Help me out here, J.R." Hunter followed him as he did his work. "I need your help. It's important to me."

"Daddy, come on." Xena smiled at him. "What will it take for you do it?"

"Dunno. But I notice there is no mention of money." J.R. gave Hunter a rather nasty grin. "If I do it, I ain't doing it for free."

Hunter's ears pointed, and his eyes dropped to the table. "I . . . um, I'm not exactly getting paid for this."

J.R. narrowed his eyes. "You expect me to believe that?"

"It's true." Hunter shrugged.

"Wait." Xena turned to face Hunter. "You're not getting paid?"

Hunter turned his gaze to the ceiling. "How many times do I have to say it? No, I'm not. The money's going straight to the police station; I'm not getting a dime."

"So all this time you've been ignoring me, and you're not even getting paid? You're just doing it for kicks?" Xena let her arms drop to her side. "Shandra's right! I must be super, ultra, mega, *uber* boring if you'd rather risk your life for no reason than to hang out with me." She kicked a chair. "I'm so stupid! How could I think someone like me could keep a guy like you?"

"Whoa, whoa. Stop." Hunter waved his hands. "Xena, is that what you think has been going on?"

"What else am I supposed to think?"

"That's not it at all."

"Then what? Why have you been so obsessed lately?"

Hunter averted his eyes, his lips pinching together. "I don't want to talk about this. Just trust me, okay?"

"No." Xena stomped her foot. "No! It is not fair, Hunter. You've blown me off, broken dates, you don't stop thinking about this job. Why? Tell me!"

"Xena . . . please . . ."

Xena glared at him. She crossed her arms and tapped her foot.

Hunter ran his hands over his hair. He stood in silence, biting his lips and his ears lying flat. His breathing shallowed. "I . . . I . . . just . . . Xena . . ."

"Hunter, you might as well tell her." Karalaina placed a hand on his shoulder. "It's not going to go away."

"I'm curious myself." J.R. said and Kathra leaned forward to hear.

"Okay." Hunter's voice cracked. He cleared his throat and took a deep breath. "Okay, here it is." He fidgeted before saying, "Before I met you, Xena, I was into some bad stuff—"

"What kind of bad stuff?" Kathra asked.

Hunter averted his eyes. "You all know I'm a bounty hunter, right? Well, a lot of those jobs . . . included . . ." He swallowed hard. "S-s-slave-finding."

The blood rushed from Xena's face, leaving her feeling cold and clammy. Her fur tingled. "A slave-finder? You? But . . . but those guys . . . I met one once . . . he almost . . ." Her voice trailed off as her voice tightened. She still remembered how her heart pounded and her body trembled the one time she had had an encounter with a slave-finder. She had been on her own when he had found her and preyed on her emotions. Then he had grabbed her and tried to drag her out of a building and into the dark night. Even now remembering how close she had been to being captured, exposed, and taken away from her family forever made her quiver inside.

"The only difference is that . . ." Hunter seemed to shrink into himself. ". . . that most of my jobs weren't completely legal."

"How do you be an illegal slave-finder?" Kathra asked.

Hunter shrunk even more. "I-i-it's hard to explain . . ."

"It's kidnappin'," J.R. said.

"I guess it's not that hard, then." Hunter forced a laugh, but he gripped the front of his shirt.

"Kidnapping?" Xena stepped away from him. "You kidnapped people? And then sold them into slavery? How could you do something like that?"

"I wasn't thinking!" Hunter gripped his hair. "I was in survival mode at the time, and I—"

"That is no excuse!" Xena grit her teeth. Her fists balled in her hands. "How could you do something so . . . evil?"

Hunter picked his eyes up. Then he ducked his head even further, and took a breath that shook his whole body.

"Xena, calm down." Karalaina patted her shoulder. "Let him finish."

"What's the point?" Xena turned her back to him, but her ears angled toward him.

"Go on, Hunter," Karalaina's soft voice cut through the tension. "Say it quick and get it over with."

Hunter took a shuddering breath, cleared his throat, and charged on. "When I decided to change my life around, I realized what a horrible thing it was that I was doing. I tried to make up for it by giving away all the money I earned illegally and sending anonymous tips to the police on where my victims were, but I knew I had to do more. So I gathered up all my information, and went to the police station and confessed."

Had Xena been looking at Hunter, she would have seen him look up and search her face before continuing. But she didn't notice. She was glaring at the floor, breathing through her teeth.

"With all the evidence I gave them," Hunter continued in a shaky voice, "they came up with 30 charges against me, but instead of taking me to trial, the DA's office, the judge, and the police cut me a deal. They said that since I was so young and since I confessed and since I had a talent for finding people, it would be better for the public, for me, and for them to work off my debt to society by doing 30 jobs for them—one for every charge they had against me. In addition to that, I had to find and pay reparations to anyone I had sold into slavery. I've been working at it ever since.

But I'm also under probation until I'm done . . . if I do anything to violate any terms of any job, I risk jail time."

He inhaled through his teeth. "This is my last job. I am so close to getting this done and putting what I did behind me. Xena . . ." He turned her around to face him. "I don't think you're boring." He gripped her shoulders and looked straight into her eyes. "You're the best thing that's ever happened to me. I want to put this all behind me so I can be with you." He gave her a gentle, almost shy smile, and his eyes shone with un-cried tears. "I want to prove that I can be worthy of you."

Xena glared at Hunter straight in the eyes. Then she turned her face away.

Hunter's hands slipped from her shoulders. "But maybe that's not possible," he said in a soft voice. He groaned softly. "I should have known better. I was stupid to think a guy like me could keep a girl like you."

Xena's ears pricked. Hadn't she said that a few moments ago? She turned to Hunter, but he had bowed his head. Tears dripped off the tip of his nose. Xena's gut wrenched as she saw him. But she didn't say anything. Only gazed at her shoes.

J.R. grunted. "Alright; I'll do it."

Hunter swung around to J.R. "You will?"

"Dun get excited. I dun want my Kid hanging around some criminal, that's all." J.R. pointed at Karalaina. "Not a word, woman!"

"I don't have to say anything," Karalaina sang as she went back to her fritters.

"Thanks, J.R." Hunter wiped his nose with his sleeve. "When do we leave?"

"Now." J.R. extended his hand to Kathra. "Can I borrow your scanner, Kitten?"

"Okay, Daddy," Kathra handed it to him.

"Don't I need to change into something else?" Hunter looked down at himself. "I think I'll be easy to spot in this."

"There's some old stuff here that should fit you." J.R. beckoned to him as he headed upstairs. Hunter trotted after him, keeping his eyes away from Xena.

Xena sank into a seat as they headed upstairs.

"Xena, are you okay?" Kathra reached over to pat her hand.

"Why am I the only one horrified by what Hunter did?" Xena

buried her face in her hands. "And why do I feel so terrible that I am?"

"Xena." Karalaina rubbed her back. "It's a lot to process. Give yourself some time."

"You guys didn't need any time!" Tears streamed down Xena's face. "Why am I such a horrible person?"

Karalaina responded, but Xena didn't hear her. All she heard was the sound of her own sobs ringing in her ears.

CHAPTER 8

"I can't believe that moron ruined my party!" Jessica stomped down one of her suite's corridors with Alex by her side. "All anyone could talk about after he left was him. They're supposed to be talking about me!"

"It was a mistake hiring him." Alex rolled his eyes. "As I could have told you at the beginning," he muttered, but aloud he said, "Shall I fire him for you?"

"No," Jessica pouted. "He'll finish the job or else! My secret is at stake."

Alex frowned. "You don't want to admit you were wrong."

Jessica glared at Alex through one eye. "Are you sassing me, Alex?"

"Sh." Alex held up his hand. "Did you hear that?" He cocked his ears.

"Hear what?"

"I heard something in your room." Alex swung open the double doors to Jessica's bedroom. In the gloom, shadows danced passed the windows. He flipped on the lights. The room looked the same as it had when they moved in that afternoon: fluttery, white curtains, large windows overlooking the beach, a king-sized canopy bed on a dais, plush, white carpets.

"There's nothing in here." Jessica pushed passed him. "Nothing but space . . . space enough to accommodate my entire entourage!"

Alex ignored her comment on the size of the suite . . . again. He'd told her several times that he had been repeating what the Isle's management told him about how many people were allowed on the Isle. No use telling her again. "I know I heard something."

"You just want to peep in my bedroom." Jessica thrust her beak in the air. "I swear, sometimes you're so stalky, I'd think you were Dan."

"I'm trying to keep you safe." Alex glowered at her.

"And you're so lippy lately." Jessica stuck her tongue out at him. "Get Taylor in here. I'm going to get out of this costume and get to bed."

"Fine." Alex turned to walk out. "I've got an appointment with the concert manager to—"

"Don't care. Just go."

Alex clenched his teeth and left the room. Soon, Alex. Soon. In a few days, he'd be able to walk away from this problem for good. He just had to be patient.

CHAPTER 9

The moon had long since set. Only the streetlights and starlight were left to keep darkness at bay.

Xena flipped over in bed so that she faced her room door and readjusted her blanket. Kathra was sleeping on the bed below, and Karalaina had retired hours ago, but Xena couldn't relax. Her mind kept replaying Hunter's words over and over. Each time she thought about what he said, her stomach flipped. But recalling how she reacted to him—how she emotionally abandoned him—felt as if someone had taken her heart, broke it in two, stomped on the pieces, and then poked them with a stick. No matter what she had done, Hunter had always been there for her. Yet the one time he had been open with her, she shut him down. How could she have done that?

"I really am a terrible person." Tears welled up in her eyes. She let them come.

A crack shot through the air.

Xena sat up in bed, her electricity flaring. She pulled it in as close as she dared and cocked her ears. "What was that?"

Footsteps. Someone rummaging downstairs. A male voice, muttering.

"Daddy? Hunter? They must be back." Xena slipped out of bed. "But what was that noise?" She tip-toed across her room, out the door, down the stairs, and peeked around the corner.

Dan.

The skunk, dressed in dark pants and a black shirt, stood in the kitchen with a bamboo tube in one hand and the bagged dart in the other.

"Hey!" Xena slapped her hands over her mouth even as Dan swung around, his green eyes catching the streetlight. Their eyes met. He snarled and spat something through the bamboo tube. It gleamed in the light, its gray feathers waving in the speed of its travel.

Xena's electricity flared. She drew it back in and then raised her hands in front of her face, knowing it wouldn't do any good. But what else could she do? Any minute now, she would feel the sting of the dart. She only hoped Kathra knew of an antidote.

But the sting never came. Xena parted her eyes. The dart's needle floated inches from her nose. It had had funneled its way through the space between her hands and hung suspended in midair between them. She stepped back, and it plinked to the ground.

Xena gazed at Dan with her mouth agape. Dan too stared, his ears drawing back.

Voices drifted in from outside—one deep and booming, the other somewhat higher. Hunter and J.R. were coming up the walkway toward the house.

"Now you're going to get it, Dan." Xena took a deep breath and screamed at the top of her lungs.

With a hiss that may have been a curse, he plowed into Xena, slamming her into the bannister. Then he snatched up the dart, ran across the house, and slipped out the sliding glass door as J.R. barged in through the front door. "Xena, what?"

"Dan!" Xena pointed at the broken sliding door.

"Stay here. Don't move!" J.R. rushed out the sliding door.

"Xena, are you alright?" Hunter dropped to his knee beside her.

"Dan was here, Hunter." Xena grabbed onto his shirt. "He broke in."

"I can see that." Hunter helped her to her feet before jogging over to examine the sliding door. "He broke this lock . . . not that it's hard to break these things. What was he doing here?"

"He came to get back the dart."

"Of course he did!" Hunter slapped his forehead with his palm. "I should have known! I'm such an idiot! Are you okay? Did he hurt you?"

Xena shook her head, but the motion sent a jab of pain through her head. "Ow!" She gripped it.

"He did hurt you." Hunter trotted over to catch her by the elbow. "I'm going to kill that flippin' moron!"

"I must have hit my head when he plowed into me." Xena let Hunter support her to the couch. "I didn't even realize I did."

"What is all this racket?" Karalaina appeared at the bottom of the stars in a sleek, light blue nightshirt. She tied a matching robe around her as she joined them. "Xena, what happened?"

"Dan broke in, Mom." Xena clutched her head. "Things happened too fast. I couldn't stop him."

"And you thought it was a good idea to try?" Karalaina stooped at her side.

Xena shrugged. "It sort of happened."

"She's got a bump at the back of her head." Hunter tapped it.

Xena winced. "Ow."

"I'll get some ice." Karalaina darted to the kitchen.

"It was really dumb of you to try and catch him." Hunter looked her straight in the eyes. "You know what he's capable of. You should have stayed upstairs and called us or the police."

"I know, but I was hoping it was you down here."

"Me?"

"I wanted to talk to you."

"About what?"

Xena ducked her head. "I was a real jerk to you, Hunter. I'm sorry."

"A jerk to *me*?" Hunter narrowed his eyes a bit. "When?"

"This evening . . . when you told us what you used to do."

"Oh. That." He averted his eyes from her.

"There you were bearing out your heart, being perfectly honest with me . . ."

"You make it sound so unmanly," Hunter muttered.

". . . and I was insensitive and cruel. It's just . . ." Xena ran her hands across the fur of her arm. ". . . what you said shocked me. You're so sweet that I would never have imagined you capable of anything like that. But I don't understand myself." She buried her face in her hands, the motion sending a jab of pain through her head. "Daddy is the most notorious criminal on the face of the planet, but I accept him no matter what he does. I don't know why

I reacted the way I did to you. I was feeling so guilty, I couldn't sleep."

"Might be the first time you couldn't justify someone else's bad behavior. I mean, J.R. raised you, and you love him. So you overlook the things he's done. But with me . . . there's no justification for what I did."

"Maybe . . . but it doesn't make what I did right."

Hunter put a hand around her shoulder. "Don't be so hard on yourself, Zizzie. I knew my past would catch up to me eventually. You're a decent girl, and I'm . . . not. Decent, I mean . . . of course, I'm not a girl." He chuckled but then fell silent. "I knew it was only a matter of time until you found out that I'm not good enough for you. But I figured being with you, even for a little while, would be worth it. And it was."

"Hunter, don't say things like that." Xena tucked her tail between her legs. "You're making me feel worse."

"You don't have to feel bad. It's all true. I've come to peace with it. Still, I have to admit, it doesn't feel nice knowing I blew it with you—"

"You didn't." Xena looked up at Hunter's face. "I mean . . . I don't want to break up with you."

Hunter's ears pricked. "You don't?"

"I want to date someone like you . . . someone who admits his mistakes and works to make it right. Rather than someone like me who thinks she's better than everyone when she's so messed up inside." Xena sniffed back tears. "I want to be your girlfriend, Hunter, but I understand if you don't want to be my boyfriend anymore."

"Xena." Hunter lifted her chin.

She looked up. In the lightening twilight, Hunter leaned close to her. Her heart jumped as she leaned in close to him. He pressed his lips to hers.

Xena's electricity danced, and she had to concentrate to keep it level. She didn't want to ruin her first real kiss electrocuting him. Still her cheeks burned.

Karalaina cleared her throat. "Here's your ice, Xena."

"Oh." Xena pulled away from him. "Forgot you were there." Her face heated even more.

"Clearly." Karalaina pressed the ice against Xena's bump.

"It took you long enough." Hunter stretched his arm on the

back of the couch. "Did you go to the arctic to retrieve it?"

"I thought I'd let you two have your moment." Karalaina sat on the arm of the couch beside Xena. "Feel better?"

Xena nodded. Pain jabbed through her head. "A little."

J.R. barged in through the sliding door. "The blasted moron got away." He paused as he took in the scene. "What happened here? Kid, why's your face all red?"

"It's not red." Xena swung her face away from Hunter.

"It's as red as a beet." J.R. flattened his ears. "And what's with the ice?"

"I'll explain later." Karalaina patted Xena's shoulder. "Help me clean up this mess, J.R."

J.R. arched an eyebrow but submitted to Karalaina's instructions, but only to get answers, he said. Xena tried to help, but Hunter and Karalaina shuffled her upstairs to bed. So Xena walked to her room with her head pounding, her heart thumping, and her eyes burning with lack of sleep. But she halted when she stepped into her room. A laugh burst out of her.

Kathra had slept throughout the entire ordeal.

CHAPTER 10

"Xena, I didn't expect you up so early," Hunter said when she came into the kitchen the next morning.

Xena yawned before taking in her surroundings. It didn't look as if someone had broken in—everything had been straightened up and fixed the way it had been before. Hunter sat at the kitchen table with a stack of papers in front of him, and J.R. leaned on the breakfast bar, drinking coffee.

"You know me, Hunter." Xena sat beside him. "I can't ever sleep in." She glanced at him, and he caught her eye. Butterflies darted around in her stomach when she remembered their kiss last night. She grinned and ducked her head.

"Still not clear on what happened after I went to catch Dan." J.R. sipped his coffee.

"Nothing." Hunter smiled to himself.

"We made up." Xena held her hands between her knees.

"Something tells me that's not all." J.R. took another sip.

"He's been trying to get the story out of me all night." Hunter picked up a sheet of paper.

"And I'll get it." J.R. grinned. "I haven't used my persuasive nature yet."

Hunter shuddered.

Xena rolled her eyes. J.R. was so overprotective. "You were

here all night? Didn't you sleep?"

"Too much to do. I gotta find Dan before he tries something like that again." Hunter motioned to the sliding door.

"I fixed the lock." J.R. sipped his coffee. "Ain't no one breaking in through there again."

"I feel safer already, Daddy." Xena grinned at him. J.R. reached over to pat her on the head before returning to his coffee. "So what did you find out yesterday?"

"That Hunter is the loudest person I've ever worked with." J.R. growled through his throat.

"I told you. That's why I needed help." Hunter picked up another paper. "I'm still sorting through all this. The only thing we had time to do was grab and run."

"Because you're so loud," J.R. grumbled.

"But I do know that Alex is getting replaced." Hunter waved a sheet of paper in the air.

"Jessica's going to fire him?" Xena took the paper.

"Looks like a mutual arrangement." Hunter rested his cheek in his hand. "Those are interview notes, and it looks like Alex set them all up."

"I'm glad it's not a horrible break." Xena stretched her arms on the table. A pen rolled away from her fur. She reached for it, and it rolled further. "Okay. That's new . . ."

"Your field must have had the same charge as the pen," Hunter said without sparing more than a glance at it. "Like charges repel each other. Man." He stretched. "I can't wait till I get this job over with. We are so far behind on your Training it's not funny. I need you to keep up with those exercises I taught you to keep your electromagnetic field under control, Xena. After we find a way to keep it permanently stable, we'll have to go back to dealing with your electricity."

"I thought we had taken care of that," Xena said.

"It's under control for now." Hunter slid another sheet of paper in front of him. "But all I've done is taught you how to hold all that electricity in. Eventually, you'll store up so much electricity that it'll have to discharge somehow—and violently. I should have had you learn how to release controlled discharges before we tackled the magnetic fields, but your field needed to be taken care of." He scratched his hair. "I am so in over my head. Your abilities are developing faster than we can control them."

Xena looked down at her fur. "So, I'm a walking time bomb?"

"Don't be silly, Xena." Hunter waved her off. "I've done the calculations over and over. At the rate you're storing electricity, you won't reach critical mass for at least another six months. Lots of time for us to get to it."

Xena ran her hands over her fur. "If you say so, Hunter."

"What the hell is this?" Hunter held up a sheet of paper. Xena decided not to comment on his language. "What the crap!" He picked up another sheet of paper. And another. "These are all death threats from Dan."

"What?" Xena snatched one of them from him. "Why didn't Jessica tell us about them?"

Hunter slammed his hands on the table. "This whole job is whacky. I can't make heads or tails of it!"

"Maybe she doesn't know." J.R. crossed his legs as he leaned. "We swiped stuff from all over the suite. Maybe someone's hidin' it from her."

"But why would they?" Xena flattened one of her ears as she looked at the note. There was something off about it . . . it wasn't quite the same as the others.

"To keep the little brat singing." J.R. shrugged. "Or maybe she does know, and it's a publicity stunt."

"Pretty deadly stunt." Hunter stroked his chin. "But for me, the real mystery is Dan. I can't wrap my head around him. He doesn't act at all like I think he will. I did my research, and his social media sites are ordinary. He's a fan of Jessica, but there's nothing there that would indicate he'd be violent. He's a world traveler, but he's never been to the Gordonian Desert. I can't get him."

"Maybe he's just crazy." Xena rested her cheek on a fist as she continued studying the note. Was it the handwriting that was off? Yes, it was a little bit different than the notes Jessica showed them. "Remember what Kathra said? The fan gets so obsessed he can't stand sharing her with anyone else."

"I dunno anymore." Hunter threw his head back. "This is making my head hurt."

"Maybe you're tryin' too hard," J.R. said.

"Trying too hard, huh? Hmm . . ." Hunter let his ears tilt back. "You know what? Let me try something." He stood. "I'll be back this afternoon."

"Where are you going?" Xena asked. She set Dan's notes and her queries aside. After all, if Hunter didn't notice anything, maybe there was nothing to notice.

"Down to the Concert Hall." Hunter grabbed his jacket. "Dan's a professional photographer, so he might have media credentials to photograph Jessica's concert. They'll be working down there to set up. I'm going to see if I can't nab him there."

J.R. grunted. "Too easy."

"I know, but instead of thinking about him as a criminal, which is getting me nowhere, I'm trying to think of him as a professional." Hunter shrugged. "The worst that could happen is I waste a few hours. I'll call you later, Z."

"Okay." Xena let Hunter kiss her cheek then watched him leave. She groaned as he closed the door behind him. "I hope he's not in over his head."

"Nah. The little Punk's got skills." J.R. set down his coffee mug. "But if he doesn't catch this guy, you know the concert's off limits."

Xena slumped her shoulders. "I know."

J.R. patted her shoulders and headed downstairs to the basement.

"I know." Xena lay her head down. "But I'm not happy about it," she muttered.

CHAPTER 11

Hunter walked into the Losierres Concert Hall with a pelican and a stork behind him. The auditorium had thousands of seats stretching in a semi-circle around the stage. Crews with ladders, microphones, cables, and other equipment milled around fixing lights and hanging props and setting up equipment. Hunter shook his head in awe. It seemed like Jessica was pulling out all the stops to make this concert and costume reveal sensational.

"Xena's gonna love this." Hunter stepped down the stairs toward the stage. He had to get Dan soon. Knowing J.R., she'd never be allowed to go to the concert with Dan on the loose.

The two birds behind him kept in step with him. They were part of the Losierres Security Team, called out thanks to a favor from Chloe.

"Thanks for coming with me, gentlemen." Hunter looked over his shoulder at them. "Like I said, it's likely to be a false alarm, but I'd rather be ready just in case. Don't feel the need to interfere until I've tagged the guy. I don't want the LST to lose their credentials and nab the wrong guy. I'll take the heat if it turns out I'm wrong."

The two nodded.

Hunter made his way onto the stage. "I don't believe it." He spotted the giant, striped tail of a skunk talking to Alex and one of the stage managers. "He's here!" He paused to stare at him. "This is too easy. Better make sure it's really him." He motioned to the

Security guards to stay back while he approached.

The proposed Dan had a camera in his hands. "And you're sure I can go up there?" He gestured to the trusses over the stage.

"They're strong enough." The stage manager nodded. "But be careful. Wear a harness or whatnot."

"I can get some real good shots from up there." Dan gazed at the truss above him.

"And I'm counting on you to do just that." Alex clapped his back and winked.

"Um, excuse me." Hunter approached them. Alex's eyes widened. He excused himself and retreated across the stage. "Are you Christopher Cutter?"

"Yeah." 'Dan' turned to Hunter and extended his hand. "What can I do for you?"

"My name is . . . is . . ." Hunter scratched his scalp. "Funny thing, I didn't expect to see you here, so I didn't decide on which alias I should give ya. So let's stick with the ol' standby. Name's Prowler."

Dan's tail stiffened. "H Prowler, the bounty hunter?"

"That's me." Hunter pointed to himself.

Dan took a step back. "What do you want with me?"

"Well, actually." Hunter clasped his hands together. "I'd like you to let me take you into custody without a big production."

"Huh?"

Hunter grabbed Dan's hand and wrenched it behind his back. "Don't struggle. You're already on my bad side for what you did last night, and I'm this close to breaking your arm for it."

"What are talking about?" Dan didn't even put up a fight. "Are you the client for the job I was supposed to do last night? I'm sorry I didn't make it, but those directions I had were bogus. When I called to find out where to go, no one would pick up."

Hunter motioned to the two Security Guards. They rushed over and handcuffed Dan.

"What is going on? What are you doing?" Dan let the two guards take him away. "Let me go!"

Hunter watched them drag Dan out. "Huh. That was easy. I thought he'd put up more of a fight."

"I-I don't believe it." Alex stepped up beside Hunter. "Christopher was Dan?"

"Yup."

"I-I'm baffled." Alex ran a hand over his hair. "He's one of our newer photographers, but he never showed an inkling of hostility toward Jessica. He has the highest satisfaction ratings, and everyone I called for a reference spoke highly of him. I knew he was a fan, but he was always so professional. I think Jessica liked him the best of all the photographers. He took amazing shots."

"Sometimes it's the one you least expect." Hunter grinned at Alex.

"I owe you an apology, Prowler. When Jessica hired you, I didn't think you could do it. But thank you for proving me wrong." Alex pumped Hunter's arm. "I can't wait to tell Jessica about this. She'll be so relieved."

"So am I now that this is all over."

"Thank you, H Prowler." Alex gave Hunter's arm one last shake. "I'm going to recommend you to all my friends."

"'Preciate that."

Alex walked off, pulling out his phone as he went.

Hunter took a deep breath. "After all that, it was this easy." He shook his head before he pulled out his phone, dialed a number, and listened to it ring. "Hey, Z. Guess what? I got him!" He pulled the phone from his ear as Xena's voice screeched. "Yeah, he was right here like I thought," he said when she settled down enough so he could speak. "I'm going to fill out the paperwork, and then I'm going to take you wherever you want to go. We are going to celebrate. I am done!"

He listened to more of her squealing excitement before they hung up. A grin spread across his face. That was it. His last assignment. He was finally free of H Prowler's grip. "Goodbye, H Prowler! I am you no more!" He waltzed out of the building. But even as the sun hit his shoulders, a dark cloud converged over his mind. He couldn't shake the feeling that he was missing something.

CHAPTER 12

Xena leaned over the bridge's railing and inhaled deep drafts of sea air. The sun had set and the sky had taken on a mauve hue. The first star peeked out of the sky. It was Friday, the day of the concert, and she was on her way with Hunter to the Losierres Concert Hall.

"You sure you don't want to sit?" Hunter motioned to the chairs. They were filled with girls and guys reclining and talking on their way to the Hall.

"I'm good standing." Xena bounced on her toes. "I'm too excited to sit still."

"So am I!" Hunter fidgeted next to her. "It's so good to be done! It was like Prowler was a beast clinging to my back, gnawing at me. But now he's gone!"

Xena examined him. Ever since he had captured Dan, he had a wide grin on his face punctuated by moments frowning concentration. The grinning won out right now. "But you liked your job, didn't you?"

"Sure I did. And I still do, but . . ." Hunter shrugged. "To me, H Prowler is the representation of all the horrible things I've done. I want to get away from him. I can make a new name for myself."

"That might not be easy."

"Don't care."

"Well, I'm glad you caught Dan." Xena hesitated before she wrapped her arms around Hunter's like she had seen Mira do to Morrin. "I'm glad I got to go with you tonight."

"So am I." Hunter turned to her. "And by the way, you look great."

All of Xena's friends had chipped in to choose her outfit for tonight. Mira had chosen a pair of eggshell white shorts that reached mid-way down her thighs. Dori had given her a light green sleeveless shirt. Shandra had lent her knee-high, white boots and told her not to scuff them. Her hair was tied back in a green ribbon thanks to Katie.

"Thanks." Xena felt the sea breeze blow through the fur on her legs. "I don't even feel uncomfortable this time."

A dark mass appeared on the horizon. It grew as they got closer until it filled the horizon. Flashing colored lights and spotlights shot into the sky, dimming the stars around it.

"There's the Concert Hall." Hunter pointed to it.

They rode the moving bridge until it deposited them onto the island. The sidewalk funneled the crowd toward the only building on the island: the Losierres Arena, a domed structure made of gray cement. The crowd jostled and pushed, each person trying to be the first in line. A reporter with yellow and pink hair interviewed certain people in the crowd.

Hunter took Xena's hand and led her around the building to a side door. Two guards, a tern and a seagull, with wings crossed barred the way. Hunter flashed his backstage pass, and they opened the door and let him in. He hung one of the passes around her neck and led her inside, putting another around his.

Backstage was nothing like Xena thought it would be. Cables and electrical cords ran all over the floor. People of all sorts with laminated cards like hanging around their necks and headphones attached to walkie-talkies on their hips, dashed to and fro, hopping over the cables as they went. Music cases and replacement instruments were stored behind the curtain leading onstage.

Hunter positioned her behind the curtain. "We can't go any further than this spot otherwise they'll see us out in the audience."

"Jessica wouldn't like that." Xena snickered. "She wants to be the only one in the spotlight."

"Exactly," Hunter said. "And they'll throw you out if you take it away from her."

"Got it." Xena gazed around from her new vantage point. Cables and cords ran all over upstage, the area furthest from the audience, but downstage, where Jessica would perform, had been cleared of clutter. Only a bottle of water had been left for her. The audience filed in, filling the thousands of seats in the audience. Mira and Shandra sat in the front row next to each other.

Xena glanced around before stepping past Hunter's imaginary line to wave at her friends. Mira waved back, but Shandra pretended not to see her. Xena hopped back over the line.

Hunter looked at her askance. "I saw that."

Xena shrugged. "Concert hasn't started yet."

"You're turning into such a rebel."

Above the stage was a web of steel crossbeams and cables. Trusses suspended by cables hanging from the crossbeams supported the light fixtures facing all directions on the stage.

"A little more around the eyes, Taylor." Jessica's voice lilted through the air.

Xena saw her by the catering table surrounded by Alex, a wolverine, a rabbit, and a heron. She wore an orange, shorts pant-suit that had been covered in sequins. Her orange boots reached past her upper thigh revealing only an inch or two of fish-net stockings between the bottom of her shorts and the top of her boots. Her body and hair feathers were green, but her hair feathers faded to a shade of blue at the ends. But her tail! Two green puffs that reminded Xena of the Regianna bird of paradise tail feathers poofed behind her. Four red feathers that looked like they hung on the ends of wires danced in the air with every movement. And then there were the five iridescent blue and green peacock feathers that waved with every movement Jessica made. Xena bit her bottom lip to stop herself from screaming. She was probably the first fan to see Jessica's new look.

Jessica caught sight of them. She sashayed over, her tail trailing behind her. "Well, well, look who's here. Prowler, and . . . Zed, is it?"

"'Sup, Jess?" Hunter jerked his chin in her direction.

"Hi, Jessica." Xena clasped her hands. "You look beautiful. Your costume is perfect."

"I know." Jessica tossed her hair. "I heard you took care of Dan for me. You have my thanks, Prowler."

"'Bout that." Hunter sniffed. "Paperwork ain't gone through."

"Talk to Fred, my lawyer." Jessica pointed to the heron over her shoulder. "He handles all of that."

"I will." Hunter crossed his arms.

"Well, concert starts soon." Jessica swung around, pivoting to compensate for her massive new tail. "Enjoy, kids. Think of it as my thanks to you." She sauntered off to her mark, backstage of center.

"You mind if I go talk to Fred?" Hunter asked Xena.

"Not at all." Xena smiled at him. "Go get Prowler off your back."

"You're the best." Hunter kissed her cheek and trotted off.

Xena watched him go before returning her gaze to Jessica. Her clothes sparkled from all the way over there, and she dragged her tail on the ground like real peacock feathers did when closed. Xena let one ear flatten. Kathra had once told her that a peacock's train could be 14% of their body weight. For a normal-sized peacock that was about . . . 28 pounds, Kathra had said. But manufactured things were always heavier than their real counterparts.

"I wonder how much Jessica's costume actually weighs," Xena wondered aloud.

"57 ½ pounds. I had to lug it all the way over here."

"Oh!" Xena swung around. She hadn't heard Alex approach.

"Sorry." Alex held up his hands. "I didn't mean to scare you. You're Zed, right? Prowler's assistant?"

"Oh. Yes." Xena stood straight.

"Thanks again for capturing Dan." Alex pumped her hands. "It's such a load off my mind."

"No problem." Xena spotted a pair of scissors in Alex's jacket pocket. They were twice the size of any pair Xena had ever seen. "Those are some scissors."

"Hm? These?" Alex held them out to her. "They're shears used for cutting cables. I was working on some backstage." He sighed. "When you're Jessica's manager, you do a little bit of everything."

"Sounds like you could use a vacation."

"Wait. I'm confused. Wasn't *this* supposed to be a vacation?" Alex chuckled. "But it's alright. This will be my last concert as her manager."

"I heard."

"Really?" Alex's face darkened. "I didn't know she was publicizing it already." He snorted through his nose and walked off without a word.

"I think I put my foot in it." Xena watched Alex walk off. "She sure is a handful." She turned her attention to Jessica.

From where she stood, if she trained her ears, Xena was able to hear Jessica running through her scales as she warmed up. She started with a low note and sang higher and higher until she hit a key that made Xena's bones quiver. "She's a handful, but man, can she sing!"

"You can say that again." Hunter put an arm around her shoulders.

"Everything set?"

"I'll have to call the police station in the morning. There's some kind of problem with the job." Hunter shook his head. "It's like Prowler doesn't want to let me go."

"Don't worry." Xena took his hand. "Tomorrow, you and I will make him."

"Thanks, Z." He pressed his cheek against hers.

Xena turned her attention to the Jessica again, glad that the darkened arena made it hard for Hunter to see her blush. It was like the air had cleared between them when Xena hadn't realized it had become congested in the first place. She grinned. She had her boyfriend by her side and stood backstage at Jessica's concert—her first one ever. Everything in her life was perfect.

CHAPTER 13

Hunter had never been one to enjoy Jessica's music, but he had to admit, the bird could perform. The sequins on her outfit sent colored dots spewing in all directions every time she moved. And that tail! It moved like a real one. And Jessica made the most of it. She shook and rattled and swung and spread it in perfect time with her music. She was a real performer.

Xena ate it up. She watched Jessica with eyes shining and hands stuck to her cheeks as if they were glued there. At the end of each song, she screamed as hard as anyone in the audience, clapping and bouncing on her toes.

Now if only Hunter could appreciate it. He wanted to. He wanted to get lost in Xena's excitement, to sing at the top of his lungs with her and dance like a madman. But . . . something pricked the back of his mind. Dan's capture had been too easy. The guy didn't even struggle. And then there was the police station's resistance to close the case. Something didn't add up.

"Jessica, you're amazing!" Xena screeched at the top of her lungs.

Hunter shook his head as the lights lowered between sets. Xena. He had to pay attention to Xena. His job was over. Prowler was gone. "You're enjoying yourself, I see."

"This is amazing, Hunter!" Xena hopped up and down. "I never want to see another concert on TV again! This has ruined me!"

"Totally different experience, huh?"

"I love it all!" Xena swung in a circle. "It's so much fun to see all the people running around back here to make it work. Like, look at those people up on those metal things." She pointed to the ceiling.

"Huh?" Hunter looked. "Must be photographers and lighting guys, but . . . they shouldn't be there during a concert."

Xena's bouncing slowed to a halt. "Hunter . . ." Her grin faded. "I hate to say this, but doesn't that guy look like Dan?" She trained a trembling finger up at the darkness above.

A black bundle crouched on the trusses. He had a device in his hands pointed at Jessica. "But . . . that can't be Dan. He's behind bars at the police station. I saw him there earlier this week." His phone vibrated. Hunter dug it out of his pocket and glanced at the screen. "It's the police station."

"Get it."

Hunter answered it. "Hello? . . . What? . . . What the-- . . . what the hell? And you're telling me this now! . . ." He listened on the other end as the music geared up for Jessica's new song. "Next time tell *me* first!" He smacked the button to hang up.

"Hunter, what's wrong?"

"That *is* Dan." Hunter stared at the shrouded figure. "They released him earlier today."

"Why?"

"He had an alibi for the attempted assault on Jessica and for when he robbed your house."

"But Hunter, if that wasn't him . . ." Xena turned her eyes to Dan. "What's he aiming at Jessica?"

Hunter hissed a curse. "Stay here." He darted further backstage. "Don't move!"

"I won't!"

Hunter dashed to one of the curtain ropes. He scaled it as fast as he could and scrambled onto the crossbeams. "Dan! Stop right there."

Dan, buckled in a safety harness, swung around to face him. "You again? Look, stay away from me."

"You would have been safer in jail, buddy!" Hunter darted toward him.

"I said, stay back!" Dan bolted away from Hunter.

Hunter tackled him to the crossbeam. But Dan wasn't so easily cowed this time. He jolted and jerked and squirmed out of Hunter's grasp.

"I'm going to have you arrested for harassment!" Dan raced toward the curtain ropes.

"If there's anything left of you to press charges!" Hunter chased after him.

Dan sprang off the beam. His harness lowered him safely onto the ground backstage. Hunter didn't have that luxury. He jumped for the curtain rope, slid halfway down, swung and leapt. He crashed into Dan.

"Hunter!" Xena rushed to him.

"What is your problem?" Dan thrashed, trying to get from under Hunter. "You're destroying my big moment!"

"It's my job to destroy the moment of would-be criminals!" Hunter wrenched his arms behind him. "I don't know how you convinced the cops to let you go—"

"Because I didn't do anything!" Dan jerked his arms from Hunter's grasp.

"But you were going to," Xena interjected. "You were trying to murder Jessica."

"You people are loony!" Dan twisted around to see them. "I'm not trying to kill her! I'm her biggest fan!"

Hunter flattened his ears. "Then what were you doing up there?"

"I was trying to expose her . . . like I was hired to do."

Hunter's ears pricked.

"It's a publicity stunt." Dan used his chin to gesture toward the stage. "At Jessica's big crescendo in the middle of 'Love Me Forever,' I activate my device. It's an override for her costume. It's programmed to display an image of what her real feathers look like over her costume."

"But why would you want to do that?" Xena said. "Why would you want to wreck her career?"

"I'm not wrecking her career. She's fed up of the lies. That's why they hired me!"

Hunter's smacked his forehead. "So many things make sense now."

"Really?" Xena flattened one of her ears. "Because I'm even more confused."

"Dan—or Christopher, rather," Hunter leaned over until he stared straight into the skunk's eyes. "Who hired you?"

"I can't reveal my backer." Dan snorted. "Non-disclosure agreement."

"Look here, you moron!" Hunter seized the fur on the back of Dan's neck. "Someone's trying to murder Jessica and has arranged for you to be the fall guy."

Dan's eyes widened. "What?"

"You mailed Jessica a bunch of notes as part of your 'publicity stunt,' didn't you?" Now that he had Dan's attention, Hunter released him. "You and your 'backer' fixed up incidents disturbing enough to raise alarms but harmless enough to be written off as a prank, yeah?"

"How did you know that?"

"You must have assumed Jessica was in on it, but she hired me to find out who's after her secret. And someone disguised as you tried to kill her once, and assaulted my girl for interfering. Now tell me, who hired you?"

"Hunter!" Xena yanked his arm. "Hunter, look! There's someone else up there!" She pointed to the place where Dan had been.

A figure in black with a bushy tail clung to one of the lines above the crossbeam over Jessica. He stretched to one of the cables supporting the beam and snipped it with a pair of stout scissors.

The cable whipped back. The jolted down, causing the other cables holding it to snap. The lights, equipment, everything suspended on the beam plummeted.

"Jessica!" Xena raced to the stage.

"Xena, no!" Hunter dove after her, but his feet tangled in Dan's harness. Xena plow into Jessica, shoving her off stage. The trusses, pars, cables, and lamps crashed down on top of her.

"No!" Hunter kicked his leg free and gaped in dumbstruck horror. In all likelihood, his girlfriend had been crushed to death before his eyes.

CHAPTER 14

The crowd thundered. Each fan flapped their arms and shrieked as Jessica geared up for her favorite part of her favorite song. She mustered up the energy emitting from the crowd and threw her voice into a crescendo. Just as she reached the peak of her performance, she would unleash her new tail and wield it around. That was sure to fling the crowd into a frenzy. She had hit her high note and was about to release off her costume, when Zed collided into her, throwing her offstage.

"Ouch!" She dropped hard on her tail, snapping pieces of it and twisting the delicate wires that held feathers in place. "What the--?" She snarled. "You little—"

Stage lights plummeted to ground, crashing onto the stage where she had been singing—where Zed was now.

Any curses vanished from Jessica's mouth. In its place blank numbness. That debris . . . that crash . . . could have killed her.

"She . . . she saved my life!"

"Jessica, come on!" Drift snatched her arm. He whisked her backstage and tossed her into her dressing room. "Stay here while I figure out what happened."

All Jessica could do was nod. Drift slammed the door, and she heard it lock behind him.

She collapsed in the plush, pink chair she had argued and cursed for, and clutched her heart. "I-I almost died tonight. I could have been slaughtered." Rage bubbled up in her. How dare the Isle be so negligent? She'd sue! She'd appear in front of all world and unmask them for the frauds they were. She'd—

She drew in a breath as her rage trickled away. What was the point? She could do that—and probably would—but if she had died tonight, she couldn't have used the money anyway. And what good did fame do when she had stared death in the face?

"Jessica, it's me. Alex." He knocked. "Let me in."

Jessica raced to the door and threw it open. "Oh, Alex!" She collapsed onto him. "Did you see what happened? Did you see how death came to claim me? Zed saved my life."

"I saw. I saw." Alex patted her back. "Come. Sit." He pulled her off of him and set her in her chair. Then he stepped back and heaved a sigh. "Oh, Jessica, you are one lucky peacock."

"I am a peahen!" Jessica watched Alex pad toward the door. "You know that."

"I also know that you must be part cat." Alex locked it. "I mean, you have nine lives."

Jessica's crest stood straight up. "Alex, what are you—"

"You just won't die." Alex turned to her, his green eyes flashing in the light. "I tried poisoning you; I tried crushing you. Nothing is working! That Prowler . . . he's good. Probably the best decision you've ever made . . . which isn't saying much."

"Alex, stop it." Jessica stood to cower against the wall. "You're frightening me."

"You won't be feeling much more from now on, you heartless vulture." Alex pulled a long chef's knife from his jacket. It gleamed in the yellow light. "I guarantee that."

CHAPTER 15

Xena curled into a ball and slapped her hands over her head. As the weight of the lighting and beams tumbled toward her, she thought, "Why am I covering my head? I'm going to get crushed anyway."

That was her last thought before hundreds of pounds of steel, cables, and glass collapsed on her. But she felt nothing. No smashing weight; no cracked bones; not even a slice from shards of glass.

She parted her eyes. The mangled mass of metal that used to be the trusses, pars, lines, and lights had encased her into a cocoon, leaving a three square foot space around her as if an invisible dome had been placed over her head.

"Whoa." Xena started to uncurl. The debris shifted. A piece of metal clanked to the floor beside her. The rest creaked and buckled.

"Don't move!" A deep and commanding voice rang through the air.

A white Alsatian—a German Shepherd, as some called them— crouched in front of her. He smiled at her . . . a smile so wide and joyous—as if all the jokes in the world were hidden there—that it settled Xena's quivering stomach.

He positioned his hands against the debris, and Xena felt electricity flare out and then contract in response to his movements. A tingling sensation, as if someone was tickling each and every strand of her fur at once, washed over her. The debris settled in place.

"Don't move, Princess." The dog looked straight into her eyes, and it was as if his head had grown to fill up Xena's entire vision. "You're in a very unstable predicament. You have to keep your field absolutely still, and for right now the only way you can do that is to remain absolutely still. Do you understand?"

Xena didn't move, but she held his eyes and willed him to realize she understood what he meant.

"I know you do." He smiled and vanished.

Xena stared at the place where he had been. She resisted the urge to shake her head or rub her eyes. Instead she concentrated on remaining motionless.

"No, no, no, no, no! Xena!" Hunter's voice slipped in through the cracks of her prison. "Xena, are you in there? Can you hear me?" His voice cracked as he called.

"Oh, no!" Mira's voice trickled in next. "That really *was* her? Xena!"

Mira? Mira was here too? Xena bit her lips together to keep from calling out to them. She didn't want to risk moving when she did. Please. Please, let them dig through this mess to find her.

"Come on! Budge!" Hunter grunted.

"That's not going to work, Hunter. It's too heavy!" Mira said. "You need something to use as leverage."

"Right. Let me see . . ."

A light shone through Xena's metal prison. She blinked and tried not to move.

"I see something! There's a cavity in there." Mira said. "Hunter, hurry!"

"Move, Mira! Let me try this!"

Xena heard the sound of metal scraping against the stage. Hunter groaned.

"Come on! Push!" Mira's voice sounded strained as if she shoving something heavy. A piece of the metal surrounding Xena moved, and Xena saw the stage to the left. "I see her!" Mira said.

Loose pieces of debris and glass clattered down, obstructing the new opening.

"No!" Hunter shouted.

"No, wait!" Mira said. "This stuff isn't that heavy." Xena heard scraping and clattering metal. Two brown, furred hands appeared, digging through the loose debris. A pair of black-furred hands, but with orange furred fingers joined them. Soon Hunter's and Mira's faces peered in.

"Xena!" Mira held her hand to her heart.

"Xena! You're alright!" Hunter heaved a sigh that ended in a smile. "Mira, hop out of the way a second. Let me pull her out." He held out his hand to her. "Take my hand!"

"It'll fall if I move," Xena said between clenched teeth.

"What?"

"If I move, it'll fall," Xena said again through her teeth.

Hunter's eyes surveyed her debris cocoon. He extended his hand and waved it around, feeling for something. His ears fell slightly, and he nodded. "Okay. Okay . . . Mira, clear the stage. Don't even let security over here."

"Got it!" Mira said, and Xena heard high-heeled footsteps clop away.

"Xena, take my hand . . . slowly." He extended it to her.

Xena stretched her hand to grab Hunter's. The debris creaked.

"Slowly," Hunter said.

Inch by inch, centimeter by centimeter, Xena reached her hand toward his. Dust showered down on her, and the debris creaked and shifted. Hunter kept his eyes on her cocoon until Xena slipped her hand into his.

He gripped it hard. "On five, I'm going to yank you out."

Xena gave the slightest grunt in acknowledgment.

"Ready?" Hunter braced his feet. "One . . . two . . ."

Hunter threw himself backwards, yanking Xena so hard it felt like her arm popped out of its socket. She collapsed in his arms. The debris crashed in after her.

"Xena!" Hunter squeezed her in a bear hug. She clung to him, feeling his trembling hands holding her. "Are you okay?" His voice quivered when he spoke.

Xena opened her mouth, but she shook too hard to speak.

"I was petrified." Hunter shifted to a seated position. "I'm so relieved you're alright."

"Xena!" Mira ran forward from across the stage. She had a smile on her face that froze when she halted to a stop. "Oh. Xena?"

"Mira!" Xena climbed to her feet. "I heard you searching for me. I can't believe you stayed here when all that stuff fell to the stage."

Mira's eyes widened as she looked at her. "Well, yeah, but . . ."

"That 'stuff' didn't just fall." Hunter clenched his teeth as he looked up at the ceiling. "When I find out who's behind this, I'm going to murder him."

"Someone sabotaged us?" Mira said, though her eyes never left Xena.

"We saw someone up there, cutting the lines with scissors . . ." One of Xena's ears flattened. Something about this seemed odd or familiar. "Or . . . no, not scissors. Shears! Hunter, I know did this. It was Alex! He must have hired Dan and told him about a publicity stunt. And he would have had access to Jessica at all times."

"Why didn't I think of that?" Hunter raced off across the stage. "Mira, take Xena home for me. I'll be back as soon as I can!"

"Yeah, but, Hunter . . ." Mira called after him. But he disappeared off the stage. "I guess that is more important than this." She turned to Xena. "But, I . . ." She trailed off.

"Mira, I'm so glad you stayed." Xena caught Mira's hands in hers. "I was so relieved when I heard your voice."

"Yeah . . ." Mira's eyes studied Xena up and down. Her brows furrowed.

"Is . . . something wrong?"

"No, sorry." Mira shook her head. "I'm trying to wrap my head around what's happening here."

"Oh, well, Dan was trying to—"

"No, no. Not that. This." Mira motioned to Xena. "How . . . how did you get your fur to do that?"

"My fur?" Xena looked down at herself. Her fur gleamed bright silver, shimmering in the arena's dim light. She hissed in a breath. Her image generator must have shorted.

"I . . ." Mira scratched her hair. "My first thought is that you're wearing an image-generator, but why would you activate it during a life or death situation?"

"I . . . um . . ." Xena's ears fell. It was over. She had lost the best friend she had ever had—she saw it in Mira's confused eyes. Worse, now all her friends would abandon her and call her a freak like they did in Justin's Ridge. Tears pooled in her ears. She backed away from Mira, turned, and dashed off the stage.

"Xena!" Mira chased after her. "Wait!"

Xena darted backstage to where Dan sat untangling himself from his harness. He took one look at Xena, and his eyes widened. He raised his camera and snapped a picture.

Her stomach dropped. First she'd nearly been killed, then lost her friends, and now she'd be exposed to the world . . . all in one night. This day couldn't get any worse.

"Need help with that harness?" A deep, growling voice rolled through the darkness. A muscular arm picked Dan up by the scruff of his neck and set him down on his feet. The other hand cleared the harness away from him.

Dan turned. His knees knocked together when J.R. stepped into the light. "Y-y-you're J.R. Dunsworth."

"Guilty. Of that and a lotta other things. Now." He placed a hand on Dan's shoulder. "You aint gonna to tell anyone you saw me, are you?"

Dan shook his head, his tail trembling.

J.R. took the camera from Dan's hands. "And ain't gonna tell anyone you saw her, either, right?" He motioned to Xena before crushing the camera in one hand.

"Of course not." Dan's tail shivered. A smell like rotting meat slithered through the air.

"Good answer." J.R. handed the broken camera back to Dan. "Go on." He jerked a thumb over his shoulder. "Bill the Isle for the camera."

Dan scurried away, tripping over his feet as he went.

"So it's true." J.R. waved his hand in front of his nose. "Skunks do squirt when they're nervous."

"Daddy!" Xena rushed into his arms. "Oh, Daddy!"

"You okay, Kid?" J.R. wrapped his arms around.

"Uncle J.R., what are you doing here?" Mira stepped over all the cables to join him.

"Kathra was watchin' the show on TV. We saw what happened so I rushed all the way over here." J.R. pulled Xena off of him. "Kid, why did you go out there? You could have gotten killed!"

"I don't know." Xena buried her face in his shirt and tried to use his bulk hide her fur from Mira. "I had to save Jessica."

"Hm." Mira pressed her lips together. "I see you aren't surprised by her fur, either. I must be the only one out of the loop."

"What about you, Munchkin?" J.R. narrowed his eyes, ignoring her comment. "Why didn't you evacuate with the rest of the audience?"

"And leave my friend all alone to be crushed?" Mira crossed her arms. "What kind of person do you think I am, Uncle J.R.? I told you I'd take care of her."

Xena closed her eyes as she pressed her face further into J.R.'s chest. How long that sentiment would last now that Mira knew the truth?

"Let's go." J.R. pulled his coat off and set it on Xena's shoulders. "Call yer Ma, Munchkin. Let her know what's happened."

"Don't you think she already knows?" Mira said, following after them. But she pulled out her phone regardless.

Xena ducked her head as J.R. led her home. Who knew such a great night could turn into such a disaster? And it was all thanks to Alex. She clenched her teeth. She hoped Hunter would sock him a good one, right in the jaw . . . for her sake.

CHAPTER 16

A knife. Alex held a knife to Jessica's throat. She swallowed hard, and it shaved feathers off her neck.

"I was hoping your death would be more dramatic." Alex heaved a great, regretful sigh. "I planned this for months. To have you mysteriously perish on the most glamorous place on earth will position you on all the front pages. Can you imagine the headlines?

"The stage crushing you was my favorite, but the poisoning at the club had a certain *je ne sais quoi* I couldn't resist. But I suppose a simple stabbing will have to do. I'll plant roses sent to you from Dan to make it look like he's gone obsessed. I even have death notes I manufactured that I can produce to the police. Everything will be perfect as long as Prowler doesn't get in my way again."

Jessica clamped her beak together and whimpered. How could this be happening to her?

"Shut it!" Alex pressed the tip of the knife to her throat. "I've heard enough of your whining." He repositioned the knife to slit her throat, and—

BAM! BAM! BAM!

"Jessica! Jessica! Open up! Is Alex in there with you?"

Jessica's eyes widened. It was Prowler.

"Him again?" Alex hissed through his teeth. "Shut up! Say nothing!" He held the knife to Jessica's throat.

"Are you sure she's there?" Prowler shouted.

"I locked her in myself!" came Drift's voice.

"Maybe she went somewhere," Taylor said.

"With the door locked?" Prowler asked.

"She's climbed out of windows before," Drift said. "She does whatever she wants."

"Oh, great. She and Alex could be anywhere by now." Prowler kicked the door. "We have to find her. Spread out. Drift, go around and see if the dressing room window's open."

"He's leaving." Alex chuckled in Jessica's ear. "Looks like he's not so bright after all."

Jessica's eyes widened. She had to do something or Alex would have her right where he wanted her. She took a deep breath and, "Help! Help! Alex is going to kill me!" she screeched at the top of her lungs.

"You little—" Alex's snarl cut off the rest of his sentence.

Something slammed into the door. Prowler and Drift were trying to break in. Jessica would be saved if she stayed alive long enough. She pinched her beak together and elbowed Alex in the stomach. He doubled over, letting the knife shift from her neck. Jessica took a step away from him before doing a step-turn, swinging her tail at him. Sixty pounds of manufactured feathers and wire slammed into Alex, knocking him to the ground. The knife flew from his grasp.

Jessica darted to open the door.

"Oh, no you don't!" Alex launched himself at her feet and tackled her to the floor. He crawled on top of her and gripped her neck in his hands. "You will die now!" He squeezed.

Jessica squirmed and wormed around, but Alex had her pinned. She looked in his eyes and saw the irony of her death written there: murdered seconds away from rescue. That would make quite the headline.

The door burst open. Drift and Prowler rushed in. Prowler dove onto Alex, knocking him off of Jessica. He wrestled Alex, but couldn't pin him until Drift stepped in. He pulled Prowler off and pinned Alex down with an elbow to the lower back.

"Jessica!" Taylor rushed in. "Are you alright?"

Jessica coughed. "No, I'm not alright. He tried to murder me! *Four* times!" "Why would anyone want to kill *me*?" Her throat throbbed where Alex has squeezed her. "I had better be able to sing after this."

"Are you kidding me, you little egomaniac? Why would anyone want to kill you?" Alex wiggled around in Drift's grasp to face her. "You're the biggest brat in music!"

"That can't be de only reason." Prowler hefted himself to his feet. "You been her manager since you discovered her. You know what a brat she is."

"But I never thought she'd fire me!" Alex snarled through his teeth.

"*That's* what dis is about?" Prowler scoffed. "Lame!"

"Give me a little more credit." Alex let Drift haul him to his feet. "Haven't you heard the saying, 'an artist is worth more dead than alive'? I've got hundreds of hours of behind-the-scenes footage, unreleased songs, exposés, and a tell-all book coming. She's worth billions when she's dead, and as her manager I'd have the rights to it all."

"But you wouldn't have those rights if she fired you," Taylor said.

Alex snorted.

"How'd you even know I was firing you?" Jessica cleared her throat and tested her voice. Still flawless.

"Maybe next time you're seeking my replacement, you don't give them *my* phone number to schedule interviews!" Alex said.

"Oh." Jessica ground her beak together. "Kathe is so fired. That's exactly what I told her *not* to do."

"Let this be a lesson to all of you she pays to torture every day. She'll be rid of you the second it's convenient. Nothing's sacred to that vain peacock."

"That's how much *you* know, Alex." Jessica hopped to her feet. "Do you know why I went around your back to hire your replacement? I was going to surprise you with a promotion when I found the right candidate. You'd be my Global PR Manager. I know that you're the one who keeps me from saying stupid things on air and manages my public persona. You're worth twice the amount I pay you, and I was going to give you just that." She placed a hand on her heart. "I'm not stupid enough to throw away my greatest treasure."

Alex's mouth dropped. "You . . . I . . ." He fell silent.

"I don't know what to say." Jessica sniffed. "I feel so betrayed." She wiped her nose in Taylor's shirt. "Drift, take him away."

"Before you do, there som'im else." Prowler stepped in front of Alex. He studied his face before punching him right in the nose. "Dat's for Zed." He leaned in close. "You lucky I dun break yer nose, but the cops dun like it when I give 'em damaged goods." He stepped aside. "Now take him."

Drift hefted Alex out.

"Well said, Prowler." Jessica gave him a golf clap.

"Jessica." Taylor wiped her shirt off with a handkerchief. "Were you really going to promote Alex? That's so sweet of you."

"Pfft! Of course not!" Jessica blew threw her beak. "He was on his way outta here. But that will give him something to think about while he's rotting in jail."

"Oh." Taylor fell silent.

Jessica swung around to Prowler. "You and Zed saved my life. Twice in one night. How can I ever repay you?"

"You can keep me and Zed's involvement outta dis." Prowlers pressed his finger against his lips. "E'ryone saw her save you, but you dun need to give details . . . like who she is or why she was backstage. Got it?"

"Got it." Jessica winked at him. "I know how to keep a secret."

"You'd better. 'Cause my job's done, which means I dun hafta keep quiet anymore. I know what you are." Prowler looked her in the eye. "So if you squeal, I squeal. You got me, chickie?"

Jessica gulped. She nodded.

"Good. Glad we gots a understandin'." Prowler shot a grin at her before sauntering out the door.

Jessica gripped her heart. After nearly being murdered twice and having a bounty hunter like Prowler threaten to reveal her secret, she needed a latte.

"Alex!" She glanced around. "Oh, right. Taylor, latte, please."

Taylor stared at her as if she had sprouted wings . . . oh, wait a minute. She did have wings.

"What?" Jessica said.

"You said . . . 'please.'"

Jessica shrugged. "I don't want to give you a reason to murder me next." She thrust her beak in the air. "Now, latte, please. Chop. Chop."

"Yes, ma'am." Taylor scurried out the door.

Jessica watched her leave as a smile spread across her beak. Her name was bound to be in all the papers in the morning. And now she'd be able to face all her adoring fans without Alex holding her back. It was all worth it.

CHAPTER 17

"I see . . . uh, huh . . . okay . . ." Chloe said into her phone. "And the tapes? Mmm, hmm."

Xena sank low on the couch, trying to hide her silver fur while listening to Chloe cover up her news debut. Hunter sat beside her, a hand on her shoulder, and Kathra sat on the floor looking up at her. Karalaina sat on her other side, and J.R. leaned on the kitchen table. But Mira . . . Mira was the one Xena tried to hide from. She stood beside the couch, staring at Xena. She had followed them back to the house where Chloe was waiting, having been notified of what happened the moment it did. Chloe spent the hours since sorting out the aftermath.

Xena peeked at Chloe over the back of the couch. Being J.R.'s sister, they shared many of the same physical features—the same sculpted jawline, same sharp ears, same piercing, brown eyes—but somehow Chloe made them look feminine. She stood tall on her high-heeled pumps with her hair pulled back in a bun, the picture of calm and purpose.

"None of those tapes had better make it off the Concert Hall. I—" Chloe paused to listen to the voice on the other end of the line. "Are you sure no one caught anything? . . . well, that's good news. Well done, you. I'll be by later, but it sounds like you handled everything like a champ. Remind me to give you a raise. Okay, Paul. Thank you." She hung up the phone. "Well, that's that."

J.R. drummed his fingers on the table. "And?"

"And everything went the way it's supposed to when something goes wrong on the Isle." Chloe sat on the couch's armrest. "As soon as the equipment collapsed, the live feed was cut. All the audience members and media was escorted out on grounds of public safety, leaving only my trusted, certified reporters on the scene. No Off-Islander saw Xena crawl out of the debris in her exposed fur."

"And what about the ones that did see me?"

"People are going to want to know what happened." Hunter rubbed Xena's arm. "You can't keep the news from reporting."

"But they're my people." Chloe smiled a warm smile that settled Xena's fur. "They're already working on a story about an outlandish, bioelectrical outfit you wear when you're working. It's also how you survived the crash. Ever since King Max unveiled his SF Emulator, people think anything's possible as long as bioelectricity is involved. They'll buy it."

"The best lies are based on truth." Hunter chuckled. "That's pretty much what went down."

"I'll have your face blurred to keep you from being recognized." Chloe stroked the fur on Xena's shoulder. "I'll say you insisted on it because of your job."

"And I do insist." Xena tried a smile.

"And what about Jessica?" Mira stopped glaring at Xena long enough to look at her mother. "How are we going to keep her quiet?"

"I've taken care of it." Hunter smirked. "She'll keep her beak shut."

"Besides, I spoke to her, and she didn't see anything significant." Chloe shrugged. "All she knows is that you saved her life."

"Thanks, Chlo." J.R. ran his hands over his hair. "I dunno what I'd do if we had to leave the Isle. I dun got 'nother place to go."

"I'm just doing my job, J.R." Chloe turned to Xena. "This isn't the worst thing that's ever happened on the Isle. These celebrities can get into so much trouble, it's unbelievable. I've become an expert at cover-ups." She stood to her feet. "I'm going to go double-check that everything is progressing properly. You coming, Mira?"

"No, Ma. I'm going to stay here for a while, if you don't mind."

Mira pinched her lips together. She returned her stare to Xena.

"You know your curfew." Chloe patted J.R.'s shoulder as she walked out. The front door opened then closed.

Xena sank lower in the couch, avoiding Mira's gaze. "Daddy, I'm sorry. I didn't mean to blow our cover."

"Ain't yer fault, Kid." J.R. grinned at her. "What you did was brave."

"Brave and a little bit stupid." Karalaina heaved a sigh. "I'm both proud and furious. What would I have done if something had happened to you?"

"I know. I'm sorry." Xena ducked her head again.

Silence fell. No one said anything more. In the silence, tapping cut through the air. Xena spotted Mira's shoes, drumming on the hardwood. She winced. Time to face the music. She took a deep breath and raised her eyes to Mira.

"Oh, so you finally look my way?" Mira snorted.

Xena steeled herself. Might as well spew it out at once. "I've been wearing an image-generator since I met you, Mira. Your mom knows about it. I've got a genetic disorder that makes me store metals in my fur. That's why it's this. The metal attracts electricity, so I'm like a walking battery. Or an electromagnet. That's why things stick to me. There are people out there who are looking for me, so we have to hide. Hunter is my Trainer. He's been teaching me to keep my electricity under control. Otherwise, I'm a danger to myself and others. So . . . there."

"And why couldn't you tell me this from the beginning?"

"I thought you wouldn't be my friend anymore."

"Seriously?" Mira clenched her fists. "Is that what you think of me? I've been the best friend to you I can be. Do you think I'd abandon you because of your fur? Do I seem that shallow to you?"

"I don't know . . ." Xena ran her hand through her hair. "All my friends in Justin's Ridge deserted me when we found out what I am. I thought everyone in the world was the same."

"That's because you've never had a friend before, Xena." Mira put a hand on her shoulder. Xena gazed at it. Mira had touched her without any fear or hesitation.

Tears pooled in Xena's eyes. She threw her arms around her Mira.

"It's okay. I knew there was a reason you were in your shell, and now I understand." Mira patted her back. "Now, then." She pulled away from Xena. "My shopping plans for you will have to drastically change. We have to highlight this gorgeous fur. It's like you're one big, silver accessory. Why would you ever want to hide it?"

"Because people have experimented on me and tried to make a weapon out of me," Xena said.

Mira burst into laughter, but paused when she saw no one else was laughing. "Wait, seriously?"

Xena shrugged.

"Munchkin, we can't let this get out." J.R. crossed his arms. "Dun even tell yer friends."

"Oh, they'd all know by now." Mira shrugged. "And everyone on the Isle will know by tomorrow."

The room plunged into silence.

Kathra looked up at her. "But Aunt Chloe said—"

"We Isle-anders can spot a phony, cover story a mile away. Every time a star does something stupid, Mama has to make one up." Mira shrugged. "Those stories are for off-Isle-anders and their media. As far as we're concerned, we keep our secrets. That's why people love coming here so much. They can be themselves without worrying."

"So no one will care about my fur?"

"'Course not. And if we let anyone visit the Isle who we doubt will keep your secrets, you'll get advanced notice."

"The Isle really is a good place to hide," Karalaina said.

"Now back to shopping plans." Mira held up Xena's hand. "The possibilities for accessorizing are endless. You'll have to put away that icky image-generator, Xena. I can see you in . . ."

"And she's off," Hunter muttered as Mira went on and on.

J.R. shook her head. "It's Chloe at sixteen."

Xena grinned at their comments but didn't take her eyes of Mira who gestured and paced as she spoke about Xena's new look. She had found a friend . . . a real friend . . . one she could be her true self with.

And that felt really good.

CHAPTER 18

"Hello, hello, hello, Kiddos! Stayf here with *Celebrity Dish*, your go to source for entertainment news and views. I'm here with pop-star, Jessica, in her first televised interview after her harrowing experience on the Isle de Losierres' Concert Hall. How are you holding up, Jessica?"

"It's lovely to see you again, Stayf. I'm hanging in there." Jessica smiled at the camera. She was sitting in the *Celebrity Dish* studio, taping an interview that would be aired later that week.

"I haven't seen you around since you went to the Isle. You've completely hidden yourself after your experience—only doing phone interviews and such. And then you come out here with this new look! And I must say, it is glorious!"

"Thank you, Stayf." Jessica flipped her hair, mostly so that her new feathers could catch the light. She was covered in metallic-colored silver, green, and blue feathers that had taken hours to glue onto her own feathers. Her tail was modelled after the Taiwan magpie, and shimmered in metallic black and blue.

"I was transformed by my experience on the Isle. Have you ever stared death in the face?" Jessica clutched Stayf's forearm for effect. "It's a traumatic experience. And to be betrayed by my own manager." She sighed as if to hold back tears. "But I was saved by a . . . get this, a silver vixen."

"Ah, yes." Stayf nodded. "I've heard quite a bit about your rescuer in the bioelectrical, silver suit. I caught a glimpse of her as they shoved us out of the Concert Hall. Unfortunately, my camera guy didn't get a shot of her."

"Suit?" Jessica blinked. "Oh, yes. Of course. Mysterious, isn't she?"

"Mysterious, indeed." Stayf rested her chin on her paw. "She's patterned herself after the Silver Foxes of legend. But I haven't been able to unearth anything else about her. Can you fill us in?"

"Sorry, Stayf. But like me, my rescuer has her secrets to keep." Jessica winked at the camera.

"I suppose I can't say more than that for now." Stayf leaned forward. "Now about what happened on the Isle—"

"I'm sorry, Jessica." A small, gray mouse stepped up to her.

"Cut, cut!" A director behind the camera sighed. "Get that mouse out of the shot."

"I'm in the middle of an interview, Ambre." Jessica turned one eye to glare at her new manager. "Go away!"

"But there's someone here to see you." Ambre pointed to the side.

"Tell them I'm busy."

"I can't," Ambre whispered.

"Of course you can." Jessica threw her hands up in the air. "That's your job."

"But look!" Ambre turned Jessica's head.

A gray vixen with raven colored hair stood at the entrance to the studio. She was surrounded by two Drymairadian Royal Guards in brown and green uniforms.

"Oh, my good golly . . ." Stayf hopped to her feet. "The queen!"

"We're going to have to reschedule, Stayf." Jessica jumped out of her chair.

"Take all the time you need. I'll wait."

Jessica rushed to the vixen as fast as her new tail would allow her. "Queen Celeste." She bowed. "What a pleasant surprise."

"I heard you were doing an interview here, so I stopped by to see you." Queen Celeste turned away to look at the studio. "I don't think I've ever been to a studio before. Everyone always comes to me. It's . . . darker than I expected."

"Yes, well . . ." Jessica grinned. "I had no idea you were a fan."

"I'm not." Queen Celeste looked down her nose at Jessica. "But I am intrigued by your new look. It is beautiful!" She leaned in close to Jessica. "Would you be so kind as to tell me about the silver, bioelectrical-suit-wearing vixen who gave you such lovely inspiration?"

"I'm doing an interview on that right now if you'd like to listen in."

"I've heard what you have to say, and that doesn't satisfy my curiosity." Queen Celeste leaned in close to whisper, "I want to know what you're not telling everyone else."

"I can't say . . ." Jessica brushed her feathers out of her eyes. "I'm sworn to secrecy."

"That's too bad." Queen Celeste twirled the ends of her hair on her finger. "It would be even worse if somehow someone found out that you are really a peacock," she said emphasizing the *k*'s.

"Peahen," Jessica muttered. Aloud she said, "I'm not sure what you're talking about . . ."

"Don't insult me." Celeste leaned in close to Jessica. "I know who you are. Would you like me to show you pictures to prove it?"

Jessica's smile faded into a grimace. "How'd you find out?"

"Please. I'm the queen." Queen Celeste tossed her hair. "Finding out something like that is cake. Now, are you going to cooperate with me?"

"Queen or not, I don't take kindly to blackmail." Jessica pouted. "If I reveal her identity, someone else will reveal mine."

"And if you don't tell me, *I* will reveal it."

"Exactly." Jessica narrowed her eyes. "If I'm screwed either way, I might as well keep my dignity. At least *she* saved my life."

"True." Queen Celeste steepled her fingers. "But if you don't tell me what you know, I won't just reveal your secret. I will ruin you. After all, I'm sure your fans will love to hear the dirt Alex spilled when he found out you had no plans on promoting him at all." She giggled. "That was a good ploy, by the way. Not only would you lose your family; you'd lose all your fans. No one will even come to church to hear you sing. And don't get me started on what peafowl community would do." She batted her eyes.

Jessica's feathers rose. She hissed in through her beak at the big, green eyes and innocent looking smile of the vixen before her.

"Fine, but let's go somewhere else. I can't let anyone know what I'm about to tell you."

"Don't worry, Jessica. You can count on me." Queen Celeste slipped her arm around Jessica's shoulder. "I won't tell a soul."

ABOUT THE AUTHOR

M.R. Anglin is an intelligent author who had no idea female peafowl were called "peahens" when she first wrote this story (though to be fair, she had no idea the species was called "peafowl," either). She has written a number of books such as, *Lucas, Guardian of Truth* and the self-published *Silver Foxes* series. Her writing has also been included in *Gods with Fur*, an anthology by FurPlanet.